MW01272921

PILLARS OF LACE

THE ANTHOLOGY OF ITALIAN-CANADIAN WOMEN WRITERS

Prose Series 46

PILLARS OF LACE

THE ANTHOLOGY OF ITALIAN-CANADIAN WOMEN WRITERS

EDITED BY MARISA DE FRANCESCHI

GUERNICA
TORONTO·BUFFALO·LANCASTER (U.K.)
1998

Copyright © The Editor, the Authors, the Translators,
and Guernica Editions Inc., 1998.
All rights reserved. The use of any part of this publication,
reproduced, transmitted in any form or by any means, electronic,
mechanical, photocopying, recording or otherwise stored in a
retrieval system, without the prior consent of the publisher is an
infringement of the copyright law.

Marisa De Franceschi, guest editor.
Guernica Editions Inc.
P.O. Box 117, Station P, Toronto (ON), Canada M5S 2S6
2250 Military Rd., Tonawanda, N.Y. 14150-6000 U.S.A.
Gazelle, Falcon House, Queen Square, Lancaster LR1 1RN U.K.

The publisher gratefully acknowledges the support of
The Canada Council for the Arts for our publishing program.

Typeset by Selina.
Printed in Canada.
Legal Deposit — Fourth Quarter.
National Library of Canada
Library of Congress Card Number: 97-78433

Canadian Cataloguing in Publication Data
Pillars of lace : the anthology of Italian-Canadian women writers
(Prose series ; 46)
ISBN 1-55071-055-9
I. Canadian literature (English) — Italian Canadian authors.
II. Canadian literature (English) — Women authors.
I. De Franceschi, Marisa. II. Series.
PS8235.W7.P54 1998 C810.8'09287 C98-900064-8
PR9197.33.W65P54 1998

CONTENTS

PREFACE

Pioneer Women in Italian-Canadian Literature

When approaching the literary production by women of Italian background writing in Canada, the contours of gender and ethnicity are inevitably adopted in the attempt of defining its fundamental character. In the context of the Italian-Canadian literary contribution by women both dimensions are twofold: the female gender role presents itself differently according to the adoption of what are commonly considered either the new or old world perspectives. Also, ethnicity is viewed as an element which, if undeniably enriching the author's cultural background, is also feared as possible hindrance for an open appreciation of her work as part of the more universal Canadian production. Gender and ethnicity strictly influence each other, defining each other's role and significance. The traditional role associated with the Italian woman is that of caregiver, and they have most of the time an important role in the passing on of the *mother* tongue and basic ways of life. Beside these obvious boundaries, others could be easily detected, such as those of time and space as determined by the immigrant experience, as one of the motifs overtly or covertly presented in this literature. Time and space are powerful variables not only in themselves, but particularly in the perception of both gender and ethnicity. Over the last decades and on both sides of the ocean, Italian women have changed their role in society as well as the way they look at their ethnic background. This is why an anthology on Italian-Canadian women writers makes sense: it can show how not simply gender and ethnicity, but also time and space have contributed to model the evolution of the feminine perspective in Italian-Canadian literature.

Several are the clichés that still affect Italian-Canadian women's perception of themselves. Usually, it has been hard for second-generation women writers to accept a cultural background which has fundamentally been disrespecful of women in their traditional and sometimes non-traditional roles. The fact that Italian culture is male-dominated has led some women to draconian refusals of their background, when, in fact, Italian women living on both sides of the ocean had to face the same sort of problems when dealing with the consequences of their changing roles, and have also tried to find similar solutions. As an example, both divorce and abortion were legalized in Italy in the 1970s. In Canada the immigrant experience sharpened the contrast between ethnicities, when, in fact, both Italian and Canadian societies are patriarchal. The space between Italy and Canada has made it difficult to perceive how time has traced its profound effects in both countries, favouring a process of women's emancipation which, to different degrees, has contributed to the Italian women's new perception of their role. For Italian-Canadian women writers the question is, therefore, not one of ethnicity, to accept or not to accept one's background; the question is how to bridge the ocean of time and space created by the immigration experience.

The Italian and Canadian shores limiting the ocean of the immigrant's inquietude cannot be simply conceived as the old and new worlds any longer. There is a long thread that bridges that ocean in a continuum, a thread made also of writings by women who in their succession show the continuity of their motifs. When did women of Italian background start to write in Canada? Well, some time ago. The first of them wrote in Italian, creating a link between the cultural and literary background of the homeland and their Canadian home. Technically, the first contribution by a woman to what is usually called the Italian literature of migration to Canada is a brief memoir written in Italian language by Anna Moroni Parken, or better, Ann Parken Moroni (*Emigranti: Quattro anni al Canada,* 1896), an English lady married to an Italian who decided to leave an account of her years as a pioneer in Muskoka towards the end of the nineteenth century.

We will have then to wait half a century in order to find a fictionalized account by a first-generation Italian woman in Canada: Elena Maccaferri Randaccio wrote three novels. Among them, *Diario di una emigrante* is a realistic and unpretentious fictionalized biography of an immigrant woman of rural background, a strong figure who is able to entrepreneurially lead her family through the uncertainties caused by the war and reach prosperity. This 'diary' is interesting because it exposes all the *angst* of the immigrant experience according to a feminine psychology and perspective. Many are the references in this novel to the unfair reality of a woman's condition at the time. In particular, her decision as an unwed mother to give her child up for adoption and continue to live in Canada on her own, represents probably the only truly feminist character depicted by a first-generation, Italian-Canadian woman writer.

If the first works by Italian women writers in Canada gave a rather factual representation of the immigrant experience, it is with the novels by Maria J. Ardizzi that a woman's experience becomes a metaphor of the universal human condition. In Ardizzi's work, realism replaces reality and the immigrant woman's condition is presented with vividness. While *Il sapore agro della mia terra* can be considered one of the most successful endeavours by Ardizzi in representing the divisive effects of migration, it is with *Made in Italy* that the dilemmas created by time, space and ethnicity are presented in all their complexity and according to a feminine perspective. Italian women are presented through a wide spectrum of figures, from the black-clad mother in Italy to the pregnant university student in Canada. Nora, the protagonist, summarizes all the ironic contradictions in an Italian woman coming to Canada, showing how time and space have contributed to shatter even further the fragments of her identity.

The idea of starting this anthology with Ardizzi is significant in many ways: apart from the literary value of her contribution, it testifies how first-generation Italian-Canadian women are not as voiceless as ordinarily thought. As we have seen, in their own way and according to their own means they have truly broken the ice for a later production that is here presented in its kaleidoscopic variety. We should look at the texts forming this anthology as a natural evolution of those first endeavours: there is a thread binding the two shores across the ocean. As De Franceschi underlines in her introduction, second-generation Italian-Canadian women writers are in the position of expressing their motifs in a different language and according to cultural patterns acquired both from their Canadian and Italian backgrounds.

The effort of putting together an anthology on Italian-Canadian women writers was timely and should be appreciated as a significant moment in Italian-Canadian literary publishing. Over the years, many works have been proof of the feminine perspective's relevance and poignancy; however, it is now through this anthology that this significance comes clearly to the foreground.

Monica Stellin

Canadian Women Writers
of Italian Origin

Women writers have been and continue to be a major shaping voice in Canadian literature. Canadian women writers of Italian descent have been publishing here and in Italy since the 1950s. Today, as *Pillars of Lace* illustrates, there exists in Canada, stretching from east to west, a bright constellation of women writers of Italian origin. In the eastern provinces, Liliane Welch, from New Brunswick, was born in Luxembourg, raised by her Italian mother. Lisa Carducci, born in Quebec is fluent in five languages and writes in French and Italian. Mary Melfi also living in Quebec, came from Italy and writes exclusively in English, which is true also of Mary di Michele. The earliest novel by an Italian Canadian woman originated from the province of Quebec, fertile ground for Italian Canadian writers of both genders, Elena Maccaferri Randaccio wrote between 1958 and the late 1970s under the pseudonyms of Elena Albani, and Elena MacRan. Both Albani and Maria Ardizzi, living in Toronto, depend upon Italian for their writing voice. Elena Albani's earliest novel, *Canada, mia seconda patria* (Canada, My Second Homeland, 1958) focuses on a young Italian Canadian family's trauma during World War II. Albani's and Ardizzi's novels view the double linguistic barriers French/English as alien signs of communication, aggravating the state of separation of self from society. Albani's novel does not directly address the predicament of the French Canadian woman of Italian origin. Nevertheless, the reader witnesses the social and cultural hardships faced by Claudia Moreni as a consequence of the mixed socio-cultural landscape existing in Quebec at that time. Claudia is a symbol of feminine tenacity and courage leaping over centuries of Italian traditions by marrying, a British-Canadian of the upper class. Like Ardizzi two decades later, Albani deals with some important considerations: linguistic and cultural displacement, a woman's isolation, the fraying of the family communication and ties. But, unlike Ardizzi's women, who remain prisoners of their longing for a life in Italy, Albani's protagonists attain the personal and social freedom in Canada that a life in Italy would have denied. Ardizzi's three novels, comprising an "immigrant cycle," display a deterministic view of life through a progressively narrowing series of choices and actions destined to lead to alienation and paralysis. The principal female characters in Ardizzi's novels are by their very awareness of being "excluded," compelled to construct for themselves a private world of illusions which provide security, but also separation.

Gianna Patriarca's poetry reveals a quest for precision of language, both Italian and English, which triggers deeply moving personal experiences. The Italian Canadian women who write in English in the 1980s and 1990s explore a variety of themes through widely contrasting points of view. The voice of the fictive persona is no longer that of the uprooted and displaced Italian immigrant, but that of integrated and acculturated Canadians of Italian descent whose primary goals are to move forward and at the same time come to terms with the traditional values of family members. From the Canadian Prairies, Caterina Loverso Edwards' *The Lion's Mouth* is set in her birth town of Venice, with some of the action taking place in Edmonton. Thus, the novel presents two worlds divided geographically and culturally, mirrored in the inner division of the protagonist Bianca. Through Bianca, Edwards explores the theme of exile and of the "other shore," dear to many Italian Canadian writers. Like Elena Albani and Maria Ardizzi, Edwards is concerned with what it means to be a Canadian with Italian roots. Like Albani's unnamed protagonist in *Diario di una emigrante* (Diary of an Immigrant Woman, 1979), and Ardizzi's Nora in *Made in Italy*, Bianca externalizes the torment of her inner life by writing. Unlike them however, she rejects a life suspended between dream and reality. Edwards' female protagonists return to Italy in search of freedom and reacquaintence with a lost past. Albani's and Ardizzi's women, on the other hand, are by their own choices compelled to remain in Canada while longing to live in Italy. They choose a passive existence in Canada based on past recollections. Albani, Ardizzi, and Edwards, whose works span four decades, focus on existential problems of Italian women in Canada, and their dilemma of loyalty to two countries, two cultures, which remain elusive to them.

Younger writers such as Mary di Michele, Mary Melfi and Liliane Welch, write poetry, the preferred genre of writers of both genders. The lyrics of Liliane (Bravi) Welch, from the Maritimes, reminiscent of her Italian

ancestral customs and traditions, dwell on remote memo-
ries engulfed by the austere nature of the east-Canadian
landscape, and by the ever-present voice of the Atlantic
Ocean. Her poetry is much appreciated precisely for its
genuine rootedness in the landscape.

The poetry of Mary Melfi is committed to exploring
men-women relationships from the point of view of Melfi's
pictorial diction which often caricatures the differences
existing between the two cultures: the Italian ancestral past
and the Canadian adopted present. The dramatic contrasts
underlying her often clinical images call attention to the
irrational that surfaces when the human psyche is unable
to weave together two disparate cultures into a harmonious
whole. Even the titles of her composition (*A Bride in Three
Acts; The Dance, the Cage and the Horse; Dialogue with the
Masks; Sex Therapy*) demonstrate this unique interest
which colours much of Melfi's very successful lyrical pro-
duction.

Di Michele's poetry examines the images of immi-
grant and non-immigrant women evidencing that most
women are unhappy with their bodies when compared to
the perfectly airbrushed female models in magazines and
posters admired by men. Di Michele conveys modern
men's perceptions of women in two celebrated mono-
logues from *Mimosa and Other Poems*. This collection also
addresses the intense experience of reverse migration,
namely, a return to homeland, a reappropriation of Italy
which for many causes a "rupture of conscience," as it has
been called. In her poem "How to kill your father," di
Michele subverts the life-death duality: the return to one's

roots which should renew and reconfirm one's physical and inner life, is turned into an opportunity for dismissing one's father, a symbolic elimination of the old that makes way for the new "Your north american education/ has taught you how to kill a father." The violent subliminal thought of patricide attacks notions of traditional patriarchy suggesting that the vision brought along from the "old world" ought to be discarded. Yet, on a less drastic note, the murderous act may also symbolize, for the younger generation of Italian Canadians, the necessity of adopting the new order of the New World with a view to integrating it with the old.

Numerous Italian Canadian writers of both genders have visited Italy following the urgings of their inner urgency voice. Their quest has been for re-acquaintance with their Italian roots on which their social and cultural life in Canada was based. A review of the motif of past time and memory, so frequently recurring in this literature, elucidates for writers, readers and fictive protagonists the often exhilarating often painful dynamics of "integration" with the culture of adoption – keeping the old while adopting the new culture — and "acculturation" — adopting the new while dismissing much of the old. Italian Canadian women writing between the 1950s and the 1970s demonstrate that acculturation is a foreign and sacrificial process which female protagonists for the most part reject. An outstanding exception is offered by Albani's very modern Claudia when, as a widow, she marries into a financially comfortable British family. On the other hand, the possibilities and advantages of cultural "integration" — coexistence with the old and the new — are openly welcomed by the Italian Canadian women writing in the 1980s and 1990s. This socio-cultural reality displayed so clearly in their fiction responds very concretely to the multicultural policies legislated in Canada in the early 1970s and mid-1980s with a view to facilitating integration for new Canadians.

Much of the writing by Italian Canadian women involves concerns with family, self, departures, arrivals — concerns inherent in the diasporic literature of Italians and of other nations as well. In addition, language — not just as a means of communication, but language that shapes identity in parallel fashion with self-disclosure — is a recurring leitmotif in the literature of Italian Canadians of both genders. In its varied inclusions, thematic interests, and vast reach, *Pillars of Lace* is an indispensable collection of Italian Canadian women's voices. It offers a stunning sample of the writers' strengths and creative styles embroidered with firm delicacy. The pieces here anthologized stir a desire for more readings and provide a lasting enjoyment of writings by Canadian women of Italian origin.

Vera F. Golini

Quebec Voices of Italian Origin

At last, *Pillars of Lace* — an anthology which highlights the writing of Canadian women of Italian origin. Those of us interested in Italian-Canadian writing have known for quite some time about the important and specific role of women who write about the Italian-Canadian experience. We have read the better known works by writers such as Caterina Edwards, Mary di Michele and Mary Melfi. Marisa De Franceschi's anthology, however, responds to several needs: first, it brings to the fore women writers who are lesser known and, second, it confirms the existence and the worth of this body of writing. *Pillars of Lace* is a groundbreaking text: it is to Italian-Canadian women's writing what Pier Giorgio Di Cicco's *Roman Candles* (1978) is to Italian-Canadian writing. In the late seventies, Di Cicco's anthology made Italian-Canadian writers visible by bringing them together within one text, thereby acknowledging the existence of Italian-Canadian literature as a corpus. Twenty years later, De Franceschi's *Pillars of Lace* encourages us to look at Italian-Canadian writing by women as a literary corpus onto itself. In previously published collections of Italian-Canadian writing the representation of works by men more often than not outweighs that of women. It is not so much that there are more men writing, but rather that their writing is more visible. Therefore, it is mostly through the man's perspective that the Italian-Canadian woman's experience has been related and read. With this anthology we have evidence of Italian-Canadian women joining forces in relating their own story, their own experience, and thereby constructing their own identity. Robert Kroetsch wrote that "we haven't got an identity until somebody tells our story. The fiction makes us real." Writing their own story makes these Italian-Canadian women even more real. This anthology shows the diversity of writing and the versatility of Canadian women of Italian descent: they are poets, novelists, playwrights, essayists and short story writers.

Women of Italian descent writing in Quebec are a very select few and belong to a very specific and complicated entity: they are touched by (at least) three cultures, a phenomenon which is represented in their writing (for example, through language interference and characterization). They represent the "other" in more than one way: they are women, they are of ethnic origin, and they write in French in a primarily English country or in English in a primarily French territory. Thus, this group of writers always writes from within a minority. Bianca Zagolin, Tiziana Beccarelli-Saad and Carol David who write in French for a primarily French-Quebecois audience are virtually unknown and unheard of outside of Quebec. Mary Melfi, Fiorella De Luca Calce and Concetta Principe write in English and therefore are not read by the French majority within Quebec.

The complexity of a multilingual and multicultural territory such as Quebec influences the writers' attempt at defining their identity and their role as artists working in Quebec. As writers they may call themselves Italian-Canadian, Italo-Quebecois, Anglo-Quebecer or simply Quebecois or Canadian. Zagolin, Beccarelli-Saad, David, Melfi, Calce and Principe are very distinct writers. They approach the same themes from very different perspectives and with unique styles. What unites them is the fact that they are of Italian descent and that they write in Quebec. Each of these writers expresses her *italianità* in a very personal way in her writing: from the presence of Italian words within the French/English text to the minor character who is of Italian origin. The degree of affinity that the writer has with her Italian heritage has a lot to do with the temporal and geographical distance from the old country and, consequently, depends on which generation of writers she belongs to. The earlier writers have a stronger link to Italy because they remember the transfer from one land to the other; Italy is therefore more prominent in their writing. Later writers, born and/or educated in Quebec can only talk about (the effects of) immigration as a second-hand experience.

Even though a writer may have a certain sensibility towards her non-francophone or non-anglophone roots, she may not want to be associated with her heritage: to be labelled an Italian-Canadian writer or an Italo-Quebecois writer is, for some, "limiting and discriminatory" or an impediment. Others feel that their Italian heritage has played a big role in their artistic development, and that their heritage is in some ways the motivation behind their writing. The Quebec writers included in *Pillars of Lace* certainly identify with their Italian roots if only by accepting to join forces with other Canadian writers of Italian descent. They seem to be aware that there is strength in unity. I applaud Marisa De Franceschi for including the translation of works by women who do not write in English (such as Zagolin, David and Beccarrelli-Saad). Language and translation are key issues in Italian-Canadian writing given that the Italian-Canadian's daily reality is influenced by Italian and/or regional dialects, English and French (in Quebec). The Italian-Canadian/Italian-Quebecois writer is constantly translating her experience in an attempt to render it accessible to herself, first and foremost, as well as to the minor (Italian) and major (Canadian, Quebecois) groups that she belongs to.

The women of Italian descent represented in this anthology have a very important role in the literary/cultural community, a role which touches Quebecers and Canadians at large. They are the voice of a very specific minority — Italian-Canadian and Italian-Quebecois women. The appearance of this anthology points to the fact that the role of Italian-Canadian women on the literary scene is shifting from a passive to a more active one. The contents of this anthology indicate that Italian-Canadian women have something worthy to say, and they possess the tools and the talent to illustrate who we are, where we come from, and how we got here.

Licia Canton

INTRODUCTION

When Antonio D'Alfonso of Guernica Editions first approached me on the possibility of putting together an anthology of Italian-Canadian Women Writers I was honoured but also intimidated by the work this would entail. I accepted the challenge with equal amounts of trepidation and excitement. The idea of being given an opportunity to search out these writers and read their work was an enticing carrot stick. With D'Alfonso and Joseph Pivato of Athabasca University providing me with lists of names and addresses, I began contacting the writers and asking for submissions. In the meantime, I scanned the libraries and bookstores for their works and read everything available. The onerous task of having to select work for this anthology followed. I did not always choose what was submitted by the authors; I sometimes found previously published work or some of their new work so compelling I simply had to showcase it here.

I must admit to another niggling fear of this project. I had for years balked at being labeled an Italian-Canadian Writer, a woman writer at that. Like so many of my fellow writers, I had always considered myself a writer, plain and simple, one who bore the tell-tale sign of the profession: a large bump on the first joint, third finger, right hand. That was the only distinguishing feature I looked for. But, after looking critically at my own work and at the work of these writers, I discovered we cannot escape our heritage, our roots. Intentionally or not, they seem to infiltrate our writing, and so be it. They add the delicate spice and flavour to our work which makes it stand apart.

What I found most interesting about the writing is its exploration of universal themes. These women do not restrict themselves to the concerns of ethnicity, womanhood, politics, morality, or any other theme. They are true writers who take on the world and address issues relevant to us all: relationships, oppression, liberty and freedom, sexuality, love, and the entire gamut of themes that make up a delicate fabric bound together by the threads of their talent.

These writers are not bound to their cultural backgrounds with rope and wire; they acknowledge their heritage and often use the images it has given them, but their intelligence makes them soar above their familiar terrain and from that vantage point they are able to see it and judge it while also being allowed to peer farther afield. They are to be congratulated for having the courage to take up the pen, never an easy highway for anyone, least of all for a woman.

I should point out that most of the writers in this anthology are published, although some of the work appearing in this book may be new, unpublished work or work previously published in French or Italian and only now available in English. Our search for good writing, however, sometimes led to the discovery of new, unpublished or recently published women writers.

The order in which the authors appear in the anthology has been roughly based on chronological age in an attempt to place these writers in the historical context and to avoid the bland alphabetical order syndrome. But I hasten to point out that this was not meticulously adhered to. For one thing, not every writer begins putting pen to paper at the same time nor for the same reasons; there are often the constraints of family and other pressures that are to be considered. I also positioned the selections to give a sense of variety in the writing, attempting to have prose follow poetry, for instance, rather than lumping similar genres together.

I would like to briefly address the title: *Pillars of Lace*. As often happens when one is a writer, an image will present itself and our inner senses tell us this is the one to use. In my case, I found myself at a posh Italian-Canadian wedding, and I use the hyphenated label since the Italian weddings I remember were not the extravagant affairs that have blossomed and bloomed in this country. Two stately, fluted Doric columns draped in cream coloured lace flanked the head table. Soft lights illuminated the columns permitting us to see the sturdy pillars beneath the delicate folds of lace. This, I thought, is *woman*. For me, the image of strength and stability is represented by the pillar. Women have traditionally been the backbone of the family. They have so often put aside their own needs and dreams in order to do their duty as wife, mother or daughter. The Lace is our other side: our femininity and vulnerability, our complexity and sensitivity. Light can penetrate lace, but it must do so according to the patterns designed in the fabric. It is a delicate yet sturdy web which drapes us, not as fragile as it seems, as anyone who has worked with lace will know. It can be intricate or simple, but it is always revealing and enticing. Whether worn or draped over an object, it clings gently. There were undertones of sexuality and sensuality in this image of the pillars beneath the lace — unintentional, perhaps, but this was, after all, a wedding, a union.

I must thank a number of people. Antonio D'Alfonso, first of all. D'Alfonso is a true renegade, a man of vision, a man whose passion spurs those around him to equal passion. He is unique on the Canadian publishing scene. He is a visionary who often sees potential where others do not and gives new writers a venue. He follows his heart and is moved by art. He is a cosmopolitan, a true tripdych: Italian, French, English. He is sometimes like a fish swimming against the current but one who always seems to beat the odds. He has given the Canadian publishing industry over twenty years of his life and, despite the tightening of the purse strings, continues to defy the odds.

I thank Antonio for his kind assistance with the selections in this book, especially with some of the new, experimental writing where he has been my guide. These selections may not in every instance reflect the taste of the editor, but I have diligently endeavoured to choose the widest possible selection of published and unpublished Italian-Canadian women writers. I have also attempted to show the many genres these writers work in. Thus, we have excerpts from novels, poetry, short stories, life writing, journalism, memoirs and other forms.

I need to thank my friends and fellow writers Margaret Haffner, Mildred Horen, and Mary Brogan for their continued support and encouragement and for their endless mission to search and destroy all typos and errors of any kind in the manuscripts. My husband, Paolo, and my wonderful son, Daniele, also need to be thanked for living for the past couple of years with an obsessed and driven woman who occasionally forgot to get dinner on the table.

Finally, I thank all the writers who patiently accompanied me on this mission. I hope I have done you honour and justice.

Marisa De Franceschi

MARIA ARDIZZI

Made in Italy

ONE

I awake in the middle of the night in the grips of some unknown malaise. From within, a familiar anguish wells up. But it is not fear: perhaps it is the heaviness of the silence which seems so full of foreboding; perhaps it is only the clash of emotions, exaggerated by the strangeness of the hour.

Long motes of time go by before I recognize where I am. The stillness of the room and the solitude in which I lie produce vague though recognizable images, distorted by the insistence of a dream that will not end. I try to give substance to the insubstantial; but the dream disintegrates into a mist, hovering lightly in the distance in a dimension I can no longer reach. There is a face which I barely recall: aunt Tina, arisen from the dead, amidst other faces of the forgotten dead.

"You never stop dying!" aunt Tina said in the dream. "And you never stop living!"

Slowly the mist dissipates; the room and its contents regain their familiar shapes and at last I begin to see myself amongst them again.

Everything is still: but I am not alone. Lately, I am never alone. Thoughts, memories, forgotten faces, they all assail me at once and lead me on along paths I have already travelled, and then they leave me stranded half-way. My memory is a storehouse into which events have been crammed like belongings into closets I no longer open. Of little consequence, really, when they happened, and yet, as I recall them, each is a link in the chain which brings me back to the present.

Of late, the past is my only companion and I tarry there stubbornly, almost as though soon, very soon, I will no longer have enough time to comprehend it in its entirety. Death could tap me on the shoulder at any moment and snip the thread of my life. I would not struggle, I would not plead; I would face the inevitable with the dignity of silence.

I have entered a dimension where time and space are unbounded: whence I came and whither I am going are questions belonging to the past and to the future: my quest for answers which I cannot give has ended in grasping onto the present.

I am almost seventy now and have acquired knowledge enough to brave the endless cycle of events ancient as time itself. A marvellous gift, that, a privilege granted by my years. I pass in review the wounds time has inflicted; I feel again the quickening pulse past hopes gave rise to; and I know once more the searing pain, as each in turn was shattered. Nothing, ever again can catch me unprepared: no illusion will deceive me anymore. I have reached the age of truth: the age which tears down institutions, which re-examines distances, which lays heights low and puts everything into its proper perspective. I await without emotion the unfolding of a play whose outcome I already know.

"You never stop dying! And you never stop living!" What can these words heard in a dream signify? Perhaps that we are dying even as we live and that we live on after death? Perhaps . . . It's true that we are dying as we live; that we live on after death in a state of which we have no knowledge is something I'd like to believe. Life is enclosed within too narrow a realm and it bestows too little for me to accept it as my only limit. Beauty imagined and never seen, flights of fancy begun and never completed, love sensed and never totally possessed . . . I want to believe in the possibility of the impossible.

Fragments of youthful readings return to mind. I remember the chest I discovered in the attic when I was ten years old. It had been bequeathed to the moths by a priest who had long ago been a member of the family. Some of the books, those bound in sheepskin and written by hand, in Latin, were the ones with which my mother preferred to light the fire in the morning. My mother never cared much for books; she never thought knowledge necessary. I saw many of those books, with their pages torn from the binding, disappear one by one under the stack of oak logs in the great black fireplace. I watched them in sorrowful stupor, accompanying the secrets that eventually formed the ashes between the embers. Those books that I had been able to save, I kept hidden in my room and I read them at night. What I managed to learn from them constituted my first peek at the world beyond the mountains and beyond the villages that slept on their summits. I was born Catholic. I cannot say how much Catholicism, in the traditional sense, remains in me from my early years. Over the years I have kept up a constant dialogue with God, sometimes rebellious, sometimes subdued. And from the fact that everything remained the same after my unburdening my- self to Him, I have come to know how distant He is and that I am free to find my path in my own way.

ဢ

If it weren't for the weight of my wasting flesh, I might believe that time has stood still. When young people speak of life and love, there are so many things I would like to say; instead I say nothing. In fact, I don't even offer advice. They chatter pretentiously about feelings and emotions as if these had originated with them. They have all the an- swers. They believe they hold dominion over the future in their own hands. I let them talk while I scan and read their minds. That which they are, I have already been; that which they must learn, I have already suffered.

I need no one as far as I am concerned. I flatter myself that I am not even old. Within me nothing has changed. Emotions and feelings are as alive as when I was twenty but there is now a deeper and more acute awareness, better than at twenty.

At my age, life has no more secrets. The truth and the deception in the human face reveal themselves clearly to me through the folds of the skin. In certain faces, I see the attempt to embellish and conceal the blemishes; behind the words, I guess the effort to hide dried-up brains and empty souls. And I can see the beauty of other faces, where beauty is truly present. In the silence I feel the dissimulated happiness and the love that is not understood. In words and voices, in sad looks and vivid glances I sense meanings that at twenty escaped me. The flow of life is full of hidden, tormented, sibilant, pleading sounds. I turn towards those sounds; I listen to them; I recognize them; I hear in them the perpetuation of life, the eternal repetition of human anguish.

I do not speak. I say nothing. To each his own experience; to each the privilege of arriving, one day, at his own destination. If I were to say that society commits a great error in silencing the old, I would be soundly ridiculed. Imagine that, they'd say, a liberation movement for senior citizens! What a quaint idea! But it's not all that idiotic, let me tell you.

I suspect that if the old don't decide very soon to organize themselves into a tightly knit group, they will be eliminated like cast-off items. In the name of love, naturally! Human beings have a particular capacity for twisting and distorting arguments in ways that will let them live at peace with their consciences. They do not know what happens in the mind and the soul of a being they label old. They will have to become old themselves to understand that one never stops suffering, hoping and above all loving, not even when, afflicted by the years and illnesses, the skin has become wrinkled and the eyes no longer sparkle.

This age which cuts one out of the human consortium and which seems to put life to rest, allows me the luxury of expressing the truth without any risks. I make use of this privilege as if it were my last obstinate form of integrity. No colour brushstrokes to hide the rotting wood of a construction in ruin; no ornaments to divert the attention from a drained body; no laughs, no gossip, no noises to fill the emptiness and the silence. Illusion has a fragile skin: I penetrate its folds, I feel its rot, I weigh its uselessness. And I say nothing. Silence, too, is my privilege.

FOUR

I am aware of a new fragrance in the air this morning: the tepid perfume of the earth which I recognize instinctively, the quivering of a season that encroaches upon another season's reluctance to die. I'd think it was a summer day if the humming of the furnace in the basement didn't reach my ears, and I know that it's too early to go out for a walk. There are things I force myself without resentment to give up, knowing that stubbornness is not strength of character. Or is it perhaps because I know that I'm no longer young?

I smile at this thought that I have had other times as well: "Is it perhaps because I know that I'm no longer young?" I'm no longer young!

Because of the mind's sophistry, the term "old" is repugnant to me; it sounds inappropriate, not at all suitable to the reality it would like to define. Objects, subjected to the wear and tear of usage become old and are thrown away. How can a living being become old, a being that, exactly because he lives, transforms himself and, in his own way, renews himself? Aging is a cruel joke that reaches only superficially its goal of deforming and deteriorating.

It is a slow, treacherous, irreversible aggression that thickens the exterior crust as drought thickens the earth: and under it, the conflicts, which have never ended, moan in the silence, timidly and jealously, as if the passing of youth meant that passions, too, have expired. The transformations which have occurred in me, in the last few years, do not seem to me to be less important or interesting than the transformation which took place from my birth to adolescence, from youth to adulthood: each transformation was different, each with a meaning and beauty of its own.

ଚ୍ଚ

Willowcrest lies flattened in the silence; the sun's rays fall with useless gaiety on the street and on the houses which seem dead. Bolted doors. Sealed windows. I don't even know the faces of many of the residents. The houses represent a transit stop, never a destination. People come and go with their belongings without taking the time to become attached to a place. The world of Willowcrest is a world that is very different from that of my youth, that noisy world without secrets, in which we entered through windows and doors that were always opened wide. The neighbourhood is made up of respectable people — respectable to the point of not offering even a glimpse of themselves, protected by middle-class respectability under which pride swarms and solitude languishes.

I recall John's ill-concealed pride when we moved here. And I never told him, in order not to destroy his joy, how indifferent I was to this or any other place, and how becoming part of the well-to-do class did not make any of us better or different.

A car emerges at the end of the street. It speeds closer, comes in the driveway with a squeal of the tires. I recognize Amelia. I wait until she rings the doorbell. And even after she has rung it, I will not immediately open the door. I will let her wait in the cold to calm the urgency with which she performs even the most insignificant task.

At times I enjoy some of my cruelties. The sound of the doorbell runs through and becomes lost in the empty house. Wait! I think to myself, guessing the impatience with which Amelia stares at the door that doesn't open. Wait! I am in no hurry to listen to your babbling. What brings her here again? Anna, of course. Hasn't she understood that Anna is stronger? Again the doorbell rings, a double ringing this time.

"I've been here for five minutes," she rails at me as I open the door. "Where were you hiding?"

Amelia wears a red dress under her coat. A necklace of shining stones reaches her stomach and bounces on her breasts with every movement. She strokes her hips and thrusts out her bosom.

"So you like it?" she asks, pointing to the dress. "It's a gift from Riccardo. He wanted to console me because I'm so unhappy these days. At times Riccardo is naive. How can he believe that a gift will make up for so many worries?"

"I like it," I interrupt her to put a quick end to the subject of her dress. The kitchen table is still cluttered with the dishes. I begin to tidy up as Amelia speaks with reserve:

"I don't want to give you the impression that I only come here to argue, but there's something which has to be cleared up between us. Well, I don't understand why you have taken a hostile position towards me. What gives you the right to side with Anna? I had expected a certain amount of cooperation from you . . ."

She is agitated as she speaks, pacing through the kitchen.

"Since yesterday, it has been impossible to talk to Anna," she continues. "I know that she came to see you but I don't know what you said to each other. She has taken up a defiant stance, obviously encouraged by someone who agrees with her. This someone is you. Do you realize the damage you do by placing yourself against me? What right do you have to approve or disapprove of the actions of my daughter?"

She rummages through her purse and takes out a pack of cigarettes. She lights a cigarette with convulsed motions. After a brief silence, she adds:

"I don't want to be rude. At your age, one commits errors in judgement unwillingly. You love Anna and forgive her everything. I know. Perhaps Anna has taken advantage of your indulgence to strengthen her stubbornness . . . Let's forget it . . . You can always make amends. You can always talk to her to remind her of the gratitude she owes her family. I've made many concessions. We have arrived at the point where Anna decides everything. Well, let her decide about her future . . . but let her give me the possibility of saving appearances. At least let the ceremony be carried out as it should . . . We're too involved in the community to turn our backs on traditions . . . A few words from you could persuade Anna to give up certain obstinate demands. It's necessary . . ."

"I'll have nothing to do with that," I interrupt her brusquely.

Amelia stiffens; she stares at me with her words hanging on her lips.

"Anna is mature enough to decide what she wants," I continue. "And you underestimate her if you think that I can influence her in some way. The decisions, right or wrong, must be hers. Anna is not rebelling against you, her family or her upbringing, as you think, but against what she doesn't believe in. There are people who want dinner served on a platter; others who prefer to struggle to earn it. I respect this second type of person: it is they who will one day know how to live with their mistakes."

"Riccardo and I have made great efforts to ensure that our children will make us proud of them," Amelia mumbles in a voice trembling with tears. "We gave them everything . . . We chose for them the best education . . . We placed them above others . . ."

"You managed to lead them by the hand until their moment of choice arrived. Did you ever suspect that Anna submitted to your will only because she had not found the courage to rebel?"

"Anna has always been docile. She never showed any unhappiness. I would have noticed . . . It must be the people she sees that made her change . . . I have the feeling that she wants to humiliate us deliberately . . . Why? Why? We've always given her everything . . ."

Amelia begins to walk back and forth through the kitchen as if burdened by a heavy weight. Suddenly she crushes the cigarette in the ashtray. She draws herself up resolutely.

"It seems that at this point there is no possibility for me to express an opinion. The only wise thing is to accept, is that right? If that is the way it must be, I ask myself what's the sense of having children . . ."

"There is no sense, as a matter of fact, if you think they belong to you . . ."

Amelia stares at me with desperation in her eyes.

"If your children don't belong to you, who does then?" she exclaims.

"No one does," I say. "Children! All that belongs to you is the agony of giving them birth, and of never owning them . . ."

Translated by Anna Maria Castrilli.

Carmen Laurenza Ziolkowski

Perfect Love

Robert Nicolas
— your enchanting
toothless smile
pre-Christmas gift.

After your birth
when perfection
was questioned
I suffered
a million deaths.

Your parents fear
my love for you
is less than
for your sister —

Have they found
a new yardstick
to measure love.

Haiku

1
A tree in my garden
houses many singing birds
life is bearable.

2
Wind whistles through
white night
Scaring tiny rabbit
Music to my soul.

3
Drops on red petals
Nightly flying angel's tears
Ambrosia for my tulips.

Progeny

Beware, woman
in the palm
of your hand
you hold
the fountain
of genes.

After the Sunset

The sun hides its face
soon twilight is upon us
flaunting colour of ripe peaches.
The horizon flames bright red
reminiscent of spilled blood.

Is it the colour of your blood, Pasolini
soaking the sand of Ostia Beach?
Your life
a continuous search —
Were you still searching?

You said:
"The night had a taste
of many future nights . . .
a poet needs time, solitude
to think, to extract forms
from the chaos of his mind."

They gave you no time
those youths,
those boys you admired, desired.

It was in the dark
after the sun hid its face
the black deed was committed.
They were many

they pulled at you
dragged you to the sand.
Was it then you said:
"Time I have no more
death comes toward me."

Sleepless Night

I fashion your face
its enigmatic smile

— we are together
side by side
on fallen pine needles
your shoulder a cushion
for my head —

the wild sea
in the distance
sings a lullaby

waves crash
on the rocky shore
in rhythm
your lips touch my hair
you whisper forbidden words —
a car speeds by
beams of light

split my dark room
and I am alone.

On the Verandah

Overlooking
frozen Lake Huron
the white haired woman
rocks
trying to remember
coaxing . . . who?
her husband, son
to enclose this favourite spot
to keep her flowers
an illusion of spring

to watch the stars
excitement of seeing
Hailey's Comet

The lens brought it too close
frightens her

she rocks faster now
weaving, recalling
long faded semblances —

Was it last summer
or ten years ago
the planets encounter
streamers. flowers
funerals, weddings —
birthdays and births —
babies crying and laughing
entangled forest of memories —

Search for Inspiration

I search for a poem
hidden among nature

In the almost dry grass
I find worms

They crawl over my fingers
my arms, my hair

I turn to lace tattered leaves
insects stroll in and out

I dig in the dust
unearth shiny white bones
I rummage through yellowed envelopes
addressed with unsteady fingers
they stare at me

I finger through ancient Thesaurus
trite words flash in my face

I fly to the moon
buried amid cosmic dust

I find a brand new poem.

Meridian

Before you arrived
an inch of snow
covered the ground
not enough to make
a snowman with carrot nose

We waited
ours hearts doing somersaults
each time a door opened

counting the hours
the minutes, and as time
wore on, the ticks of the clock.
The sun
travelled to its meridian
and you, Alexandra
were presented to us
like a bouquet of pink flowers.

Decadence

Labyrinth of cold offices
raw turkey in plastic bags
toilets rank
with cigarette butts

slim bodies with masked faces
fat men wooing young girls
nude babies too old for their ages
a pit of snakes
coiled around
a faded globe of earth.

Rendevous with Love

Heart pounding
I wait for darkened house
to sleep
like a thief I sneak away

soft carpet
of the front lawn
muffles my hurried footsteps
shaded path is my accomplice
night shadows my guides

newborn moon plays hide and seek
as I run to reach tryst
and my faceless love —

We talk, we hug, we kiss
our fingers interlaced
he smells of fresh cut grass and violets

a strong remembrance
of dancing moon
split in a thousand pieces
in the pail of water
as he offered me a drink
I have forgotten his face and his name.

PENNY PETRONE

Breaking the Mould

CHAPTER EIGHT

When the priest slid the grating open in the dark confessional box of St. Andrew's Church, I began to whisper, "Bless me, Father, for I have sinned. I confess to Almighty God, and to you, Father." St. Andrew's stood at the top of Algoma Street Hill. I felt little and safe beneath its massive columns and arches, its high, slender stained glass windows, its beautifully sculptured wooden pulpit. Watching over me from above were the brightly painted figures of the eight Canadian martyrs: the Jesuit Fathers, Brebeuf, and Lalemant, Chabanel, Daniel, Garnier, Goupil, Jogues and de La Lande. I often meditated on their sufferings at the hands of the Iroquois as I did the Stations of the Cross.

I chose St. Andrew's for confession because the Jesuits in charge did not know me. I sat in the dark pew examining my conscience, trying hard to find sins to confess, and to remember the exact number of times I had told a fib or had "unclean thoughts," whatever that meant.

Sins were categorized as mortal or venial. Mortal sins were grievous and were punished by direct descent into Hell, that terrible place where after death one burned to a crisp for all eternity. Failing to observe the fast on Holy Days of Obligation and missing Mass on Sundays were mortal sins. I recall running up Bay Street hill and down Banning Street to get to Mass before the Gospel started, in order for the Mass to count. Otherwise, I would have to stay for another Mass.

Venial sins were minor offenses such as talking back to parents, telling white lies or losing one's temper. They merited Purgatory, the waiting room for Heaven where the soul burned until it was absolutely clean. My little world was filled with fear and dread.

When I felt that I had examined my conscience sufficiently, I chose the box of a confessor who didn't speak too loudly; I would have been mortified if his voice were heard by the other penitents waiting in line. I went behind the deep velvet drapes and knelt in the dark. The grate opened. The priest murmured the words of the prescribed ritual. I recited my confession. Sometimes his manner would scare me into hiding a sin. Then I would plan on confessing it another time and to another confessor. Finally he spoke: "For your penance say three *Our Fathers* and three *Hail Marys*." The grate closed. I had to be on my guard not to sin before receiving Communion the next morning. Nor could I eat, or drink water, after Midnight.

At Mass I couldn't wait to receive the body of Jesus. When the sacred moment came, with eyes downcast and hands clasped, I walked in procession to the altar. The priest put the Host on my tongue. I was afraid to swallow the thin wafer that so mysteriously held the body and blood of Jesus Christ. I was careful not to chew it. If it got stuck on the roof of my mouth, I cautiously licked it off. In absolute union with my God I walked back to my pew.

With eyes closed, I sat silently conversing with Him, humbly beseeching Him to help me through my problems. I pledged Him my heart. And it felt good.

Catholics were not supposed to enter a Protestant Church, because in those days the teachings of other faiths were considered heresy. And yet, as a youngster I started going to Sunday School at Bay Street United Church, where the neighbourhood kids went on Sunday afternoons. I liked singing "Jesus Loves Me" and looking at the coloured illustrations of Bible stories. There was no storytelling for kids at the Catholic Church. Besides, the Rev. Mr. Simpson and Mrs. Simpson were so nice to me. Once, they sent us a box of toys with pieces missing here and there. I told Mamma they came from the Rev. Mr. and Mrs. Simpson. Mrs. Simpson? Could a priest have a wife? Mamma tried to keep me away after that. Surely, the Simpsons would think me ungrateful. After all, they had sent us presents.

It was Mamma's faith and example which inspired and guided me in the Roman Catholic faith. I grew up in an atmosphere of prayer and the strict observance of church discipline. Daddy left religion to Mamma. Like the typical Southern Italian male he regarded religious observances and churchgoing as *cose femminile* (women's things).

St. Anthony's Church at the corner of Banning and Dufferin was our parish church. It was here that Mamma felt at home when she arrived from Calabria. It was here she heard the familiar Latin and her native tongue.

St. Anthony's has since burned down. But, when I was a child, it was a wondrous place of candles, flowers and incense and lots of statues. There was Anthony, patron saint of the church, holding the Baby Jesus; Joseph, patron of work and the working man, holding a sheaf of lilies; Barbara, patron of good weather, and Mary, of the Immaculate Conception, with her small bare foot crushing a serpent. In the centre of the high altar was Jesus, with a flaming red heart pierced with thorns exposed on his chest, and his arms wide open, embracing the whole congregation.

Many of the statues were surrounded with lights set in elaborate filigree. There was a marble communion rail and a sanctuary light in the shape of a heart. When the lights went on and the candles flickered, my young eyes were filled with wonder at the beauty of it all. When a bell tinkled, announcing the entrance of the priest, the whole congregation arose to participate in the dramatic re-enactment of the Last Supper — the sacrifice of the Mass. When the priest intoned the "Asperges me" and proceeded up and down the aisles to sprinkle the congregation with holy water, I felt blessed if a drop or two fell on me. St. Anthony's Church was my sanctuary, my shelter against the harshness of school and the tensions at home.

Year after year, the same rituals were important to me. They gave me pleasure and security: the Masses with their beautiful Gregorian chants, the Benediction of the Blessed Sacrament, the Forty Hours' Adoration, the litanies and novenas. I enjoyed reciting the same prayers over and over again: the Latin prayer composed by St. Thomas

Aquinas, *Pange lingua gloriosi / Corporis mysterium / Sanguinisque pretiosi* (Sing, my tongue, the Saviour's glory. Of His flesh, the mystery sing); and the prayer composed by St. Ignatius Loyola: "Soul of Christ, sanctify me. / Body of Christ, save me. / Blood of Christ, fill me. / Water from the side of Christ, wash me. / Passion of Christ, strengthen me." I can still hear the priest intoning each line in slowly measured syllables.

In those wonderful days of faith that marked my childhood and adolescence, I loved the Lenten and Christmas rituals best. On Ash Wednesday, the priest dabbed ashes on our foreheads with the reminder, "Ashes you are and to ashes you will return." On Holy Thursday, the ladies of the Altar Society took great pride in beautifying the Altar of Repose. I recall my eyes feasting on the altar resplendent with Easter lilies and candlelight. Mamma used to go late in the night to keep Our Lord company in his final hours.

The next day, Good Friday, was the saddest day of the year for me. At church, no candles were lit; no organ was played; no bells were rung or holy communion given. At home Mamma would not allow us to play. It was a day of mourning. At three o'clock in the afternoon I would make the Stations of the Cross and meditate on Christ's selfless love for us, even unto death. Oh how sorry I felt for my sins which had helped crucify my Lord. My ingratitude shamed me. I pleaded, "Jesus, my Lord, my God, my all, how can I love Thee as I ought?"

Many years later on a blistering hot day in Jerusalem I recited the same plea and made the Stations of the Cross with four hundred students from the Sorbonne in Paris, walking from Pilate's Palace to the crucifixion site at Calvary. The students were barefoot and three of them carried heavy wooden crosses. As we slowly edged our way along the narrow Via Dolorosa, in the very footsteps Our Lord had trod nearly two thousand years ago, I marvelled at the piety of the young pilgrims. As for my own devotion, I found my attention straying to the painted red toenails of the girls.

I remember getting up very very early on Holy Saturday to attend the solemn ceremonies which fascinated me: the blessing of the new fire, the paschal candles and the holy water. My Chicago cousin, Rose Elia, remembers that when the bells tolled the end of Lent, her mother lay on the floor, her arms stretched out to thrash away the evil spirits, and recited, *"Uscite serpente della casa mia, che e risurcitato il Signore mio"* (Depart evil spirits from my house because my Saviour is risen).

The rock rolled away from the tomb and the triumph over death is a mystery that the years would interpret, but a new-born Holy Babe was cause for immediate joy. It meant feasts and carols, joyful family gatherings and special religious services. When, as children, we were allowed to go to Midnight Mass on Christmas Eve, we felt we were the luckiest kids in the world. Mamma made sure that we arrived early because it was one time of the year our little church was packed to the doors.

The church at Christmas was a festival of flaming poinsettias and dazzling light. The enormous elevated *Presepio* (manger scene) with its figures of the Holy Family, the shepherds, the Magi and the barnyard animals was built at one end of the altar and surrounded by evergreen trees. The fragrance of pine and the sweet pungency of incense floated through the air. From the choir loft, the trumpets of the organ burst into jubilant peals. And the angelic voices of my cousins, Agatha and Carmen Sisco, and Frank Covello, sang to greet the new born child: "Angels we have heard on high," "O Holy Night," "Adeste fedelis." And we waited in quiet reverence for the magic of the midnight hour.

Mamma was piously raised in the Roman Catholic faith, but medieval superstitions with which she had grown up in Calabria, lingered. Much as she sought to repress them, she feared them. The *mal'occhio* (the evil eye), for instance, was attracted to beauty, excellence, strength and wealth. Its dread gaze had the power to inflict all sorts of misfortune. And she feared the *affascino,* the spell which an envious person casts upon his or her victim. She showed me how to make the traditional defense against the evil eye by pointing the sign of the horn made with the thumb tucked under the second and third fingers, with the first and fourth fingers extended, and saying, *"Fare mal'occhio"* (Go away, evil eye). Although her habitual expressions to undo the possible malevolence were pious phrases such as *"Benedica"* (God bless) or "Madonna mia, aiutame" (Mother of God, help me) or *"Madonna mia, duname forza"* (Mother of God, give me strength), I have heard her say, on occasion, *"Non ci capisi lu mal'occhio"* (May the evil eye not strike).

Mamma was wont to rejoice at other people's suc-
cesses and say, *"Chi Dio ti benedica"* (God bless you) or
"Beato u latte che t'ha dato mammata" (Blessed be the milk
that your mother gave you), or *"Beato le minne chi ti hanno
allatato"* (Blessed be the breasts that suckled you).

Mamma's belief in the protective power of the saints
was strong: St. Anthony recovered lost articles; Christo-
pher protected travellers; Roch healed sores. On February
3, each year Mamma took us to church to have our throats
blessed with two crossed candles and to ask for the inter-
cession of St. Blaise who had saved a child from choking to
death on a fishbone. On December 13, she honoured Lucy,
patron saint of eyesight. There was reason for this. I was
short-sighted, had worn glasses since Grade Vl11 when
the school nurse informed me I had myopia. I had com-
plained to Mamma that this was caused by a defect in the
eye's construction, that it was hereditary, and could not be
cured. She decided to get supernatural help and invoked
St. Lucy's aid. One year, she made a novena to her, culmi-
nating in visits to the homes of a few friends to solicit funds
for a High Mass to be sung in Lucy's honour. So sincere
was she that, in keeping with Catholic tradition, she hum-
bled herself by going barefoot into the homes. According to
legend Lucy is honoured among virgin martyrs because
she plucked out her beautiful eyes in order to preserve her
virginity and her eyesight was miraculously restored. In art
she is depicted holding two eyeballs on a tray.

As added protection, Mamma wore the brown scapu-
lar of Our Lady of Mount Carmel and a number of miracu-
lous medals in a little pouch attached to her brassiere with

a safety pin. Often she would forget to unfasten the pouch before her undergarment was washed, so the scapular and medals went into the washing machine.

Mamma was especially devoted to Our Lady, the Blessed Virgin Mary, honoured by Roman Catholics worldwide as the Seat of Wisdom, Gate of Heaven, and Refuge of Sinners, and the most powerful of saints in interceding with God who refuses nothing to His mother.

Each year on July 16, Our Lady of Mount Carmel's feast day, Mamma took several hours, no matter how busy she was, to spend with Our Lady in private adoration. The Sisco family had special devotion to Our Lady of Mount Carmel, because as an eight-year-old, Mamma's brother, Giovanni, who had been told not to go near the water, disobeyed and was caught in a whirlpool. He called on Our Lady of Mount Carmel and miraculously found himself on shore. From the time she was a young lady, Mamma never failed to honour the debt the Sisco family owed to Our Lady of Mount Carmel.

The salvation of her immortal soul was Mamma's spiritual goal in life. She made novenas to Our Lady of Pompeii, and, from the age of nineteen, she devoted an hour, between two and three in the afternoon on the 23rd of each month, to the recitation of the Rosary, to gain the grace of a happy death.

Each year, on December 4, Mamma would be "at home" to her friends who would gather to celebrate the feast day of St. Barbara, the patron saint of her town. Oh, how busy she would be on that day, making *panetelli,* little loaves of St. Barbara's bread, and other baked delicacies.

She would set the table with a white tablecloth and nap-
kins, trays of sliced cheeses, father's homemade meats,
bowls of green olives and of dried black olives that had
been soaked in oil and oregano. At the end of the meal she
would serve her own homemade brandied cherries which
she kept stored in jars for years at a time. When I came
home from school, the aroma of coffee filled the air.
Mamma was happy. All was well in the world.

Florence Perrella

Prologue to the Poems

In my dreams, I travel a lot —
walking, talking, guiltily smoking cigarettes.
But when I wake, I have A.L.S.
There's nothing I can do for myself —
like an infant, I depend upon others to survive.
First, there were my four children,
my ex-husband, and family care workers from the C.L.S.C.
Now, in addition, there are the doctors, nurses,
support staff and volunteers of the Palliative Care Unit
of the Royal Victoria Hospital here in Montreal, Quebec.
I have entered a merciful, if sometimes frustrating world.

Basil and Clementines

1
Pink sky and two small lavender clouds.
A butter milk wash floods my window.
Blue sky and green leaves transfigured by light.
Six o'clock: the nurses turn me over.
Adriana empties the trash, Ivo vacuums the hall.
The kitchen courier delivers her menus.

2
July

A pot of Basil on the windowsill
hides the white chimney,
the suggestion of Ligurian hills
masks the odour of ashes.
The weather is torrid —
if I fail to pay attention
my basil will wilt, wither and dry.

3
Hilvette feeds me.
She was up last night
celebrating Christmas.
Hilvette says every month has a colour.
The colour of July is brown. Like her.

4
For a grandchild, I'd recommend orange —
pure as pureed carrots,
warm and thick as sweet potatoes,
lethal as mushrooms
(you have to pay attention)
fresh as a splash of clementine.

5
Now lemon verbena divides the light
with basil and a potted orange tree.
Dr. Benoit suggests

I put down tiny sheep to graze
my windowsill Versailles.

6
The woman next door
has cleared useless objects
from her room. Her bed in the corner
is pushed against the wall. She refuses to eat
and everyday there is a little less of her.

7
I was giddy because the weather was fine
and at the museum, no one had to pay.
We ate on the terrace and laughed
at the Symbolist's obsession with death.
Mary felt the baby move and she
fed the sparrows sugar pie.
We got back to the hospital in time to attend
a wedding in the solarium.

8
August

Three friends came to visit —
one brought a pretty nightgown,
two read an entertaining story,
three gave me the gift of her hands.
She is knitting a blanket for the grandchild
"A meditation," she calls it.

9
My daughter is like the Theotakos.
She has made of herself a universe
to house a divine being.
How you float among the stars, child
careless of your supremacy.

10
We consult the books for names,
combining them for consonance and connotation,
testing them for ridicule in the schoolyard.
Only one is perfect.
Someday, it will be your turn to name us.
You will work at it all of your life.

11
First, urgent need drove me to words.
Then, desire for ever narrowing subtleties.
Now, urgent need drives me to mute fury and tears.
There are some that say, "Silence is eloquence."

12
There was a bouquet on the front door.
It meant Grandpa had died and people could visit.
He was on the long table in the cold front parlour
where Grandma usually made her ravioli.
The men sat with him and the women served
homemade cherry brandy. No one slept.
In the morning, more people came. Aunt Julia
hung me over the coffin and said, "Kiss him,

he's sleeping," Her lie was annoying,
but he was cruel. He never opened his eyes.

13
On Wednesday afternoons,
there is "Happy Hour" in the solarium
wine and cheese, cakes and tea.
I come in my wheelchair, some come in their beds
to hear the man from Peru play on his hand carved harp
and his companion sing with her small sweet voice
and well practised gestures.

14
Even the most simple life
finds comfort in order.
To read in the morning
rest in the afternoon
and entertain at night
is not without meaning.

15
There is eloquence in silence.
Indeed, there is fullness in void.
In a word,
there is meaning
when doing nothing at all.
If the ego were only less clamorous.

16
Suddenly, wind rocks the branches,
craggy clouds hide the innocent sky
and cast their shadows on the mountain.
Suddenly, the student nurses and
young doctor
are gone. I lose my
craving for iced tea,
put on a cardigan and close the window.

17
A newborn's tremulous cry
shook the foundations of night,
I heard a man recite the creed.
It was not a dream —
A child was baptised across the hall
In her dying mother's arms.

18
They spoke of her fabulous name
and her proud professional past,
as if to recall her dignity.
She was too old for words,
She had only one gesture left —
To stretch out one hand in communion,
and with the other, hide her eyes in shame.

19
I call her "sister,"
since both of us hang by the teeth,

but she, who sings me songs
and gives me messages for God,
has the advantage of wings.

20
Someone offers me lunch —
I say, "First the neck brace off."
I try to spell it with a chart and a straw between my teeth,
but he mistakes "collar off" for "colour of"
and offers me a spoonful of orange.
It's a very little problem compared to other's.
They've offered to double my Prozac.

21
Her gentle hands wash me,
her fragrant creams soothe my skin.
His friendly eyes hold me,
his sentences bind my wounds.

22
September

One day, Annie and I went on a baby chase.
Into the Women's Pavilion and straight
to the birthing centre. We lie,
"Just checking the space for our sister,"
But no babies were there and
the nursery on postpartum was dry,
since all the babies were well
and sleeping with their mothers.

So we spied
through a crack in a bedroom
door and found our prize
no bigger than a goose berry
and wrapped in white lace,
"Ahhh."

23
Autumn is a time for pruning,
and I who know there's good in losing,
grieve to say, "Good bye."
Jacques, the volunteer
(who claims to know nothing)
is moving to the forest
to pose his questions to the wind
and hear the answers of the birds.

24
I celebrate the new year in September,
when glacier blue marries blazing orange,
when abundant earth gives birth to culture,
and Emma Perrella gave birth to me.

25
Memory is a far soprano
a voice that carried on the wind,
and memory is a mute communion
like marrow hugging bone.

26
Someone placed it in my room
without a noise —
it's scent was my awakening
a white rose poised
in fullest opening
and deep repose.

27
She had her baby with her
and seventy seven Italian cousins.
Their stories, jokes and cries of despair
filled the corridors and all the rooms
as if everyone must take part in the tragedy.
Next door an old French Buddhist was tended
by his pretty young bride from Nepal.
She shut the door in vain, for silence.
In the morning she returned with incense.
Its fragrance filled the corridors and all the rooms.

28
For Christmas
September, Continued

I looked out the window
and grey glared back.
A cloud had occupied the Mountain,
and below,
the invisible city wept.

29
For a few minutes
on certain days
the sun magnifies a stone
below the lintel.
Its hard beauty terrifies me.
A raven dives and soars
strafing my window.
Only I can see the end of the blue space.
Hear the thud and crack of bone.

30
Florence means flower
and Perrella, a matrilineal name,
means son or daughter of Pietra.
Pietra means stone.
I am the daughter of stone.
How many tears will it take
to raise a flower from stone?

31
The stony path —
I meditate, but fail to reach
detachment —
I threw up three times last night,
at war with my computer.

32
"Don't worry, I won't die —
I'll take care of the kids."

He nearly died this year of cancer,
but I believe him.
We used to be married.
Now he enters my room in the dark
to speak from his heart,
or sit up and watch
'till I fall asleep.

33
Jem and I are going to see the colours
up north in the town of Val David.
We'll sit near the lake as red and yellow
flames flicker on the water.

34
The bears have come to town —
they are knocking at the front door,
pounding at the rear,
peering through the shutters,
tearing up the porch —
It was a very bad year for blueberries.

35
A congregation of geese
veering south;
a shower of yellow leaves
drifting across the lawn;
an old man bending to pick
one leaf that strikes his fancy.

36
We met her last year.
She wags her head, "you're failing."
I can't reply.
She warns, "I hope you're praying!"
I want to tell her about the computer —
"you're going through the dark night of the soul."
I had no idea.

37
October

Nurse Diane hears me thinking,
but can't discern the words.
She turns up the radio
to cover up the noise.

38
I've been wasting my dying
on frivolous things . . .
I would suffer for others
if I suffered at all . . .
but I'm loved and I know it.
Can I offer God this happiness?

39
A tree on my windowsill
like a child's drawing,
full of orange polka dots.
They smell like tangerines

but taste like lemons, and
we've all had our sour bite
save Annie, who's studded hers with cloves
and made a pomander to scent her clothes.

40
In an hour the world will know
what took a year to deliberate —
did he kill his wife and her lover?
and if the verdict is "yes,"
are people in such need of a hero
they will say, "Civilisation is depraved —"
and bring down the city with him?
Or the verdict is "no"
will they be resentful,
say, "Justice can be bought —"
and sink deeper into their skins?
This much is certain, many will say,
"He's guilty but beautiful, we forgive him."

41
There are fingerprints on this film —
you have cut it apart and put it together
so many times, you hate it before the first showing.
Let me assure you, it's survived your contempt,
it is one of a kind, a work of art —
your fingerprint is on it.

42

In a pink city on a mountaintop,
Francis walked to the town stare,
took off his clothes and said,
"I am a child of God."
I've always loved him for that.
I lie in my bed, blanket to chin,
but find it impossible to hide.
All are aware of my tantrums and sulks.
My bowel movements and odours are writ
down and discussed, but I too am a child of God.

43

Martin comes into my room in the dark
with a white lacy flower he picked in the park
saying, "What are you doing in bed so soon?
Stay up with me and watch TV."

44

Last May, when I tried out a head set
to drive my wheel chair,
I did figure eights in the hall.
On Friday, when it was installed,
it took all of my strength
to move just a few inches.

45

On Saturday, we celebrated
Anne Jeanette's wedding.
Mirrors covered the walls

of the banquet hall
and I could not ignore
(to my shame)
I stood out from all the rest,
my chin propped up upon my chest.

46
On Sunday, I went home for Thanksgiving dinner.
The boys had fresh haircuts and all wore new clothes.
Jerry gave thanks that we were still together.
(We were a heavenly but fragile host.)
Later, they brought a desk from the basement to put in
     my room.
There was a line in the rug where my bed used to be.
(This was a weekend of seeing my ghost.)

47
The day Annie showed me her X-rays
I marvelled over her beautiful bones,
Her proud, "Winged Victory" hips.
I couldn't see the pain.
Did I never see —
asking her too often, too soon
to bear me aloft?

48
Ellen took me out for a walk because
the savoury smell of fallen leaves,
the warm sun and cool breeze,
the brave gold banners

on the trees insisted.
Ellen said, "See the children playing!"
and in the dishevelled garden, "Feel these leaves,
they call them 'lambs ears,' and smell
the cat's mint — that's what it's called, isn't it —
cat's mint? You wont have another day like this one.
It's a shame. Tomorrow, they say, it's going to rain."

49
Just beyond my childhood streets
Islamic settlers have built
a Casbah of the mind.
I'd bring the children there
after school and buy them treats,
but they find it far to walk,
even in a dream.

50
On the Boulevard of Palladiums and Monuments
I ride my bicycle past buildings
in the classical style, graceful, yet
each one a distinct surprise from the last.
It has recently rained,
there are puddles between the fountains
and reflecting pools, but not a sound.
There are neither people nor trees,
nor anything that breathes.
Just the whiz, whiz, whiz of my bicycle wheels.

51
I saw my Grandmother come back from the dead
to spend a long weekend at the Jersey shore.
She was happy and fit, and made the suggestion
we stop off for bread at the delicatessen.

52
I dream of Annie and Jem,
round as Easter eggs in their coveralls.
They still wear their souls on their faces —
I hover, I kneel, I press
small toys in their dimpled hands
and send them out to play.

53
And here is my Uncle Lou,
alive and cooking in Grandma's kitchen.
I tell him about Martin and Jem,
too bad they haven't met,
for they are fine cooks too.
Wouldn't he enjoy their company
now that they are grown.

54
Quebec is building an Arc
to shelter his own.
But when the deluge comes,
will Yahweh close the door behind us?

55
They let in a draft of cut flowers,
a funereal scent which alerted me
to the serious nature of their visit.
Dom Laurence read from Saint John,
"I am going to prepare a place for you —"
We meditated in silence, "Maranatha."
Then Polly read from the Gita, "He thinks
he is slaughtered but the spirit is forever."
Dom Laurence blessed me, thanked me,
waved his cap in the air like a friend from the shore —
I am at peace.
I don't want to scream anymore.

56
Her screams break free
from pain becoming song,
hymns of praise
to her Saviour and Lord.

57
Since I cannot move or talk,
I finish old business by
making moral choices
in my dreams.

58
Mary placed my hand on her belly
and someone tapped, tapped, "Hello."
(I imagined a slender heel.)

I wanted to play "Little Piggy"
with your toes, but not yet.
You'll be fatter in December,
the coldest months are to come.
Mary placed my hand on her womb.
I felt the curve of your shoulder
imagined you in your bath,
but I can wait until December
(it is the darkest month)
to see your light fill up the room.

59
Breathless Louise said it at breakfast,
"This is the first day of snow —"
(It wasn't a blizzard,
just a powder on the grass.)
Bright eyed Magda announced it at noon,
"This is the first day of snow —"
the memory of unvarnished youth,
and the shiver of our pagan past.

60
I want to hold my firstborn, Mary,
sing her to a carefree sleep
one more time. I could easier guide
powdery wings to rest on a flower,
or cradle the phosphors in the sea.
Mary, you were named for the Mother of God —
forgive weakness, draw on her strength.

61
God comes as a child
to make lovers and dreamers of us all.
God comes as a child
to remind us that we're always beginning.
God comes as a child
to promise we'll be born again.

LILIANE WELCH

A Sense of Voice

The rapid taps of my father's walking cane punctuated my outings with him in the Luxembourg forests when I was a child. They set the pace for a fast trot, an almost military step. When no one was within earshot my father burst into hiking songs and expected me to sing with him. The majestic oak and beech trees where old Celtic mysteries still shivered would resound with the thunder of his voice, and the border stones between France and Luxembourg along our path disappeared. He also liked to drill me in breathing exercises. "Deeply in, strongly out," he commanded. This was supposed to strengthen the lungs. "You will never be a fine soldier," he said, casting a strict, male judgement onto all girls and women who were in his eyes *arm Ge'ster*, "poor souls."

Next to these "poor souls" there figures prominently in my father's menagerie of human derelicts the *Fatzerten,* "the ragpeople." Anyone was a *Fatzert* who walked through the streets of our town with unpolished shoes, who was entertaining "adventurous" relations with members of the opposite sex, who belonged to the Communist Party or to a labour union. Any conduct different from his own qualified others as *Fatzerten*: wearing blue jeans in town, boys and girls talking together unchaperoned, children answering back to grown-ups, or, worse, questioning the priests and nuns during Catechism lessons.

When it came to religion there was no grace for deviants in my father's book: not living literally by the Ten Commandments and all the prescriptions of the Catholic Church turned one not only into a *Fatzert*, but cast one immediately into any of the other ranks of miscreants — the linguistically juicy *Knaschterten* or "dirtmugs," the primal *Drecksäck* or "mudsacks," the lascivious *Houerejeëren* or "whorechasers," the aromatic *Fuurzbeidelen* or "fartbags."

When, as a child, I had to march next to him through the cathedral-like forests with well-polished shoes, immaculate in my blue velvet coat and bonnet, listening to his pronouncements about breathing correctly, studying ardently and obeying elders, I looked with envious eyes onto the *Fatzerten*, who ran through the woods with dirty shoes and played in the streets at dusk while I had to go to church for evening services.

At home we lived always in the shadow of my father's disapprovals and feared his unpredictable rage-tantrums. These sporadic volcanic eruptions could be provoked by anything: a coat not hung correctly on its hook, fingers unwashed, a return ten minutes late. During these outbursts, while he flew at my mother, the stoic witness of the storms, I would often creep upstairs into my room to read. I would cover my ears with my hands in order not to hear the word-thunder from below.

At the dinner table my father reviewed regularly all the *Fatzerten* who had run over his path that day. These inspections were only interrupted by: "Eat faster!," "Sit up straight!," "Don't act like a *Dabo* (a 'nitwit')!" And now and then, when my brother and I ignored his theatrics, his hand rapped the table with a tap similar to that of the walking cane in the woods, this being the sign for our bodies to bolt into an upright, rigid stance.

There were times, however, when we children would escape from the paternal drills. Twice each winter my maternal grandmother left her farm and came to our house for extended visits. The letter announcing her arrival filled the house with the free air of her fields. I was sent to get her at the railroad station because my mother didn't want to be seen walking through the streets with a farm woman who never conformed to wearing fashionable clothes. Soon after my grandmother was in the house, a hatmaker appeared to try on her a new hat which would accompany the slender, short woman home, three weeks later, in a shiny hat box. During the summers, vacationing in her kingdom of vineyards, fields and animals, I sometimes went into her bedroom to peep into the massive oak wardrobe. On the top shelf were piled neatly all the hats my mother had bought her — they rested peacefully and unworn in their hat cemetery.

Walking home from the railroad station, holding my grandmother's large hand, I walked in the light of the guardian angel who looked down at me every day from his painting above my bed. With my grandmother's appearance, the beam of that painted angel became understandable to me in a bodily way. Her steady country voice with its rolled *r*'s and musical cadences enwrapped me immediately in a vast mantle of primordial words, a shield of earthbound images which became for three weeks a magic talisman against the paternal tyrannies.

Looking at the slight, small woman one would have never detected the powerful will behind the benevolent grey eyes shining from the unpretentious face. The same determined perseverance that governed her farm and raised four kids without a husband, stood up to my father when he trespassed on her domain to woo my mother. My grandmother accepted him, as husband to her daughter and father of her grandchildren, but she never welcomed him as an equal. Early on in the game she bluntly told him while they were tying up vines, "Here you'll always be an outsider," thus assigning him an immutable place in her geography of fellow humans. And the outsider never dared to address her during her lifetime with the familiar "you." For more than fifty years he used the formal "You" of distance and respect.

My father was born and raised fifty kilometers further North in Méischdrëf, a small village hugging the Sauer River, on the border between Luxembourg and Germany. A hilly land of woods and thickets, its atmosphere is more misted than that of the broad-faced, sunbathed southern Luxembourg where my grandmother's farm stood. The northern people were less clear-sighted than the southern-ers and more easily overwhelmed by the yoke and wizardry of the Church and, hence, more prone to fitful authoritari-anism or childlike obedience. They were in some sense wilder, less "civilized." My father's childhood memories returned frequently to his swimming exploits in the Sauer

River. His own father had been killed by a falling tree when my father was only six years old. His mother was known for eating regularly two pounds of white lump sugar while walking ten kilometers over to Germany to visit relatives.

For the southerners, whose vocabulary was studded with "Luxembourgified" French words and whose manners were more "romanic" owing to the century-long ties of intermarriage and labour contracts with France, the "germanic" northerners like my father were headstrong, brutish and vulgar. They tolerated no contradiction and bore within them a rage that erupted unexpectedly — a mark of all uncultured, instinct-driven tribes. They were related to the barbaric northern hoards whose invasions had spelled the doom of the Roman Empire.

More importantly, however, the heroine of Luxembourg's most original fable was a country mouse — Mouse Kätti; she hailed from Bermereng, my grandmother's village. Mouse Kätti's wisdom was definitely southern. She had a manner of vigilant and attentive meditation, gave her life to the ground and dedicated her descendants to it. Hers was an ancient, intimate familiarity with her land, like that of my grandmother's. My father's roars and shouts, on the other hand, were not part of that life-style. After one of their violent word battles, I heard my grandmother refer to my father as "that vicious lion," "that fiendish tiger." She also never quite forgave my mother for having defected to the city with a northerner.

After we had eaten, when my mother and I did the dishes in the adjoining kitchen, my father remained at the table in the dining room with the old farm matriarch. Then the word contests between them began. Through the stone walls came the firm, fervent voice of my grandmother. Talking, she would pick up the breadcrumbs from the tablecloth and face steadfast and inscrutable the mounting holler of the man who to her was a bellicose and depraved child and woman suppressor. They "discussed" everything and agreed on nothing. My grandmother never lost her calm, and her saintly forthrightness lent her convictions — on village politics, national figures, weather conditions, childraising principles — an unassailable mood of truth against which my father's roars battled in vain. He always stormed out of the dining room with eyes flashing from a blood-red face. My grandmother emerged composed as the fields and meadows of southern Luxembourg, as a figure in a Cézanne painting. She radiated the ambience of her own native landscape where, as I knew from my summer vacations, all beings floated transfigured on the grass and the earth lay in the light of another world, its ground shaped and cultivated through centuries of human labour.

For me the two worlds speaking out of those two voices already adumbrated my later life in words. My grandmother's ancestral world was measured by a solitary interaction with the earth. She had earned her freedom of spirit, sober resistance and grave nobility through hard agricultural labours. Equal to any man, in her fields she had given the ground an occasion to manifest its benevolence through the work of her hands. With a vigilant attention, an expert will, she had worked with impulsive farm animals. With deliberate gestures, she had cared for her vines in all seasons, cutting, cleaning and dressing them with an art legated to her by the Romans who had already worked her vineyards at the dawn of historic times. Her strong-willed courage and powerful wisdom stemmed from these incessant, solitary, silent tasks. To her animals she spoke in a low, patient voice. Slightly raised when addressed to humans, the voice echoed the discipline received from the taciturn earth. Her life was a pious calendar; its words were the images of a Holy Scripture put into motion by the sun in the sky, the rain on her fields.

The best part of the day for me during my grandmother's visits came at bedtime. Sitting next to me on my bed, under the beam of the guardian angel on the wall, she held my hand in hers and improvised prayers radically more compelling than those of the priests and my parents. The vibrations of her voice conjured up a space in which all saints and God himself spoke as natural phenomena. These rhythmical litanies, punctuated by the incantational recurrences of divine and natural names, sanctified language and made me experience for the first time the miracle of a secular transcendence. An instinctive repulsion from the institutional representatives of God on this earth made me recite the evening prayers with my mother as a dutiful routine where the mind wandered. For those six weeks each year, however, my grandmother's voice grounded me in a sacred magic, a marvellous creation devoid of the dry flatulence of priestly sermons.

My father's speech bore all the tensions of the early twentieth century European transfer from the rural lands to the urban centers. From his youth on a farm he had retained only the habits of rising early and cultivating a vegetable garden. Paradoxically, he moved easily into the corporate organizations of towns. His office job in the steel mills regulated his existence. Since he was not a solitary consciousness, the rules imposed on him by the bourgeois society of the adopted city life never bothered him. A public man, he felt at ease in urban crowds, he enjoyed going to cafés, to funerals, to dinners, to large gatherings. The great peace and calm of the fields which his voice must have known as a child, had vanished behind the sharp and irritable utterances of city outbursts.

Although there must have been, in times gone by, a common source, for me no connection existed between the two worlds of these antecedents of mine. Even though I had not yet decided whether I would become a lone poet or an urban organizer, my grandmother's voice with its solitary contemplation of the earth, with its penetrating mysteries, exerted a primal fascination over my young mind. My father's exhortations and judgements which saw moral transgressions everywhere, the haste and rage of his utterances, made me experience claustrophobic suffocation.

There is no photograph of my father and my grand-mother together. The vowels of the fields would not mingle with the consonants of the town. The earth-breath of the meadows and the engine-clang of the steel mills remained antagonists to the end. My grandmother's words had made love with each acre of her land; my father's rehearsed the urban impatience to overcome such archaic intimacy. At ninety-six, my grandmother's voice had the clear, intense ring of a bell. When I saw her last she said, "Your father was not your friend. You speak like me."

Books:
Prohibitions and Celebrations

Already before I could read, the sight of books entranced me. Holding one of them in my hands filled me with delight. Later the sound of their letters entered my ears. What I loved was enshrined in them. Their images were my instructors: curving me away from the activities of priests, nuns and the approach of boredom; bringing me within an understanding of what might be revealed by a sunbeam on a mountain peak; telling me to spend time alone so that I should enjoy being alone without fear; opening up a broad sense of life with room in it for all creatures and many loves.

In 1943 when I entered primary school in Luxembourg, the world of literature was divided into two: good books and bad books, clean or useful ones and frivolous or dirty ones. Once a week a nun taught us the Bible, one of the good books. I was desperately bored. Through the words of that virginal woman the life of Jesus unfolded insipid and hollow. I preferred to make up my own fairy tales. After a few lessons I asked, "Was Jesus always a good person?" The nun's suspended gesture and her immediate rebuke, "You're irreverent to our Saviour," spurred me on to increased impudence. When the nun then tried to persuade me that the New Testament was the world's greatest book of adventure, I cried indignantly, "Adventure! That's just dumb saints with halos round their heads!"

The nun gave up, resented me and regarded me as ill-bred, a troublemaker. So did her colleague, the priest who taught us Catechism lessons once a week. While the Bible bored me, the Catechism unleashed in me a bottomless distrust for books that were "useful and good." I subjected the priest incessantly to a stubborn questioning. He soon instructed my parents to correct my irritating ways. My father pontificated, "If you don't obey the priest and memorize the Catechism you'll become a cleaning woman in the hospital emptying bedpans, or in the mines scrubbing toilets." That didn't scare me because I had befriended old Reuter, a miner whose hand I used to hold when, as a small child, I walked him home from work, and I liked a charwoman who lived down the street.

After World War II, my hometown, Esch-sur-Alzette, Luxembourg's major mining and steel centre with a population of 25,000, harboured three convents, one Franciscan monastery, three parish churches the size of North-American cathedrals, and two smaller churches on its outskirts. On any day you could encounter swarms of priests and nuns ambling through the streets dressed in their long black puffy robes. As a child I always felt their presence and surveillance. Twenty-five years later the convents were empty and God's servants had disappeared.

On the streets I gave the priests and nuns a wide berth. I did not like the sermons. I disliked their long black garments as well. They were not thin and spiritual, they were voluminous and dumb. I stepped up my inquisitorial challenges against their teachings at school. Above all I could not conceal my hatred for the Catechism, that grave-yard of rules and regulations which had to be memorized under threat of physical punishment. Whenever I asked a question, the priest turned to stone and declared, "You blaspheme again! You'll go straight to hell when you die!" At home my father thundered, "She's a heathen!" and reproached my mother: "You have no authority. She'll be the shame of the family, a gypsy!"

Meanwhile, religious instruction continued obligato-rily up through my high-school days. The Catechism, a veritable door to darkness of my youth, consisted primarily of negativities; it established all the "shalts" and "shalt-nots": You were not allowed to lie, to steal, to kill, to covet thy neighbour's wife. You were not permitted to wear indecent clothes, to have lascivious thoughts, to speak with boys unattended. Not only were you forbidden to read "dirty" books, you were also ordered to pray regularly, to go to confession, to love God, your neighbour and your par-ents. This book of threats and commands, filled with una-tonable sins, reminded you of all the horrible deeds you might commit if Jesus or the Virgin Mary would not inter-vene to save you. I preferred the Latin songs we sang in Church. I couldn't understand their words, but I lost my-self in their rhythms and sounds.

My distaste for the Church has lingered ever since. Its Catechism made God appear as an evil tyrant who control-led all life, especially children. My first notions of power stem from that book. I have never been able to hear the Catholic dogma without connecting it to suppression. Of all the Church's misdeeds, however, the most dreadful, in my eyes, was the debasing of literature. Like all young schoolchildren in Luxembourg I carried in my linguistic baggage the word *Index*. For us, this mythic tomb of condemnations enshrined such forbidden and venomous morsels as "Voltaire," "The Marquis de Sade," *The Flowers of Evil*. Only in high-school did I learn that "Voltaire," the name of the famous blasphemer, was not the title of a book.

Every week my mother sent me to the *papéterie* to fetch a Swiss magazine to which she subscribed. One day on my way home our priest, a dark suspicion in his eye, tore the magazine out of my hand, examined it and snapped, "Trash!" He didn't confiscate it; I ran home and tossed the magazine on the table with the words, "Trash! So says our priest." My mother immediately fought like a lioness for her weekly novel installments and for the documentaries about exotic lands. My father, who regarded the Church as absolute and ever-lasting, found the right line to belittle such frivolous and suspect literature: "Boring stuff!" Here I felt the existence of a living evil. I saw the priest and my father as villains imposing themselves with malicious satisfaction between my mother and her elementary love of the written word.

Immediately after the war, when I was eight, the Red Cross sent me, with a convoy of undernourished northern European children, to a Swiss family to be fattened up for three months. Protestant Switzerland, with the yet inexplicable call from its mountain peaks, filled me with wonder. The people were not oppressed, the food was delicious, the landscape dramatic, no priests appeared on the streets.

Switzerland also brought an acquaintance with my first adventure books, *Globi in the Jungle, Globi's Adventures in America*. A documentation by image and rhymed verse of a legendary beast's world travels, these stilled my yearning for an innocent knowledge which rendered the priests' threats inoffensive. I loved these books rapturously and continued to buy their yearly installments upon my return to Luxembourg. Not a day passed without my leafing through them. I lived in them, swallowed what I read. They filled me with hope. I carried them to school on my back. They belonged to me, they were my icons. Their stories were the miracles of my life. Globi, the world trotter with the black beret, became an heroic figure, a benefactor of mankind. Books, ever after, exerted an infinite fascination over me. I didn't care whether they were good or bad, I had fallen in love with the pulse of letters. From the moment I read them, no priest had power over me, no shouts from my father had meaning.

My yearnings for a new social order and for distant lands, however, received their definitive direction when the books of the German author Karl May entered my life at about ten years of age. Like a glutton I devoured the wildness of Winnetou, the Apachee chief. Finally, I had found in May's Far West a landscape where the natural order prevailed, the societal one not yet having been established. In this utopia the values of the Church didn't count; everyone fended for himself, stood on his own merit. Freedom-drunk, I located myself on May's pages, immersed myself in an exotic paradise of unlimited adventure. I have never forgotten the Indians riding across the solitary, wide

American spaces. Here I consorted with heroes, lean, wild
and taciturn, with noble beings. Their names and deeds
overwhelmed me and presented an effective escape from
the *Index*-world of the Catechism.

From that time on, the conflict between Old World
and New World became a crucial tension for me and the
compulsion to keep them separate never let me go. I
dreamed of emigrating to America and of making my life
there. To my mother's dismay I often announced my in-
tention to the people I talked with on my daily rounds
through our town. It was also Winnetou who led me to
read Hemingway and Steinbeck. Daily cohortation with
the latters' adventurers and hoboes impelled me at sixteen
to apply for an exchange student scholarship to the United
States.

The impact of all those books shaped me even after I
did emigrate at eighteen to the New World. My initial
university years in Montana were dominated by omnivo-
rous reading of American writers. Melville, Faulkner,
Whitman provided an angle on my new locations which
made them doubly resonant. When, a few years later, in
those same Rocky Mountains, I met the man who became
my life companion, his first sentence sufficed to show me
at once that his concerns, like mine, were rooted in the
reality of books. Instantly, we were inseparably bound
together. In the darkness of a cosmic night, amidst thou-
sands of other beings, I could have recognized in his words
my sister soul. Our vocabulary, arising from books, was
witness to a communality of interests which continues to

persist outside or inside them, in the realities they rehearse.
It is the basis of our well-being and life together.

Tapping Reality

I come to myself in writing poems and in climbing mountains. These two activities hold out the promise of a new world, of a life still fresh and innocent, of an adventurous and solitary plenitude. In both, I am grabbed by the quiver one can experience when approaching for a fleeting moment the face of the sacred unveiled. In both, dream and action become reconciled and join on a spiritual summit. Poems and mountains are paths toward knowledge and fulfillment.

Early mornings I sit at my table in my Sackville cedar house. I write as the earth begins to stir. Through the unknown spaces of that outside I try to find an orientation as the writing touches the ground and casts me into an adventure every bit as severe and ritualistic as an alpine climb. As my pen moves over the white, empty page, a gaping void opens up; the same abyss along which my feet hesitate on an exposed mountainous traversal. My words tap reality to decipher its sounds the way my hands slap the stone for secure holds when I climb. The words become seismographs; like the hands they want to catch the smallest noise.

Poetry, that long itinerary, that inexhaustible exploration, guides me over the difficult routes of life like its twin, climbing. Both drive me early summer dawns outside toward some summit. The huge masterpieces of nature are yet bathed in prehistoric light, their torsos evoking the geological cataclysm which engraved them onto rock and void. As my feet invent a climbing route over unknown terrain and as my arms clasp the rock tightly, a different rhythm pulses through the body, the simplest gestures and things cease to be ordinary, a magical plenitude has transformed them. After hours of precise labour the same unsayable exultation hoists me onto the peak, as the crazy joy which seizes me when the final words complete a poem.

Writing and climbing push me to seek and apprehend, incite me to meditate; both are measures for life, tests, lessons, itineraries. They elicit prudence and courage, hubris and humility, discipline and freedom. A sacramental energy evolves from event to revelation. When from their void the rocks and from their silence the words respond to my questions, then all existential contradictions have become resolved. Guido Rey, the Italian climber, said, "The combat with the mountain is useful like a labour, noble like an art, beautiful like a faith." Writing poems is a similar event, it too involves a potential action, a visceral passion for what it means to be alive, and like all heroic upsurges it pulses with a light, neither masculine nor feminine, which addresses us in what we might be as human beings.

Diptych

Each August Departure from Europe

Packing the suitcase, my feet remain
in Luxembourg's streets. It's busy, but the cafés
spill heady scents and light fires in restless heads,
summer spreading to a wide land of friendship.
Crowds herd the sidewalks all day. Bells,
palpable from the cathedral's roof, reclaim
what used to be real. Right here history flows,
a current carried by these blended silts,
blessed when cities cascade and families
go raspberry picking. At the Halifax airport
I shall forget this world like a dress
returned to its armoire. But its silks
will ravish me during January nights.
Canada's silence wrapped tight around me.

All winter in Canada

Surprises. Hallelujahs. Cups of wind.
Horizons to frighten us, or to beseech.
Days for islands, and for scrawled dreams.
Hours so weighted with golden coins
we walk knees bent, triumphant.
A cathedral navigating angels
and miracles home through the dark.
Dogs that take us to those woods, we might

never venture into. Open seas, the kind
that becomes souvenirs. Ice-motes in spring.
Worn out letters. Stories that travel alongside
a hidden river. Voices we pray to
but that remain in the trees. A people's magic and
necessary passwords, perhaps ours.

Winter Storm

On that January night
I waited in my study for a phone call,
Watching the blizzard close down our house
And thought about bashing the narcotic
Of conventional life — becoming a beggar,
A professional without special talents,
A conquistador discovering
A temple, gold fire in my mouth! —
Meanwhile on CBC
A Dr. Love cast melancholy over the room,
Reporting that despite mammographies
Breast cancer is epidemic
In the western world. Floodlights outside
Broke the snow
Into golden flecks that filled my eyes;
Alternately shaken by the snowplough's
Thud and the yellow lights refracting
The dark sky, my stare kept
The emptiness passable.

So I felt at home, with that winter storm,
Committing follies in the sanctuary of reason,
While steel prows swooshed
Big waves of whiteness over my mind.
Relaxed because I knew even the pheasants
Wouldn't work tomorrow in the woods,
All schools uninhabitable,
Three Maritime provinces on their duffs.
It made your joints dream
You were a bear wrapped in drowse,
Curled up to a partner
While your fur grew thicker
In the warm underground den.

That night, as the phone wouldn't ring,
During my search for heaven on earth,
Bridges between humans and beasts,
Changes of costumes and skin, I put on
My grandmother like a flying robe,
Trembled backward directly above the heart —
Her pewtery eyes called the roll of all dreams
Before holy images,
The wind, *enfant terrible*, grew fiercer . . .
I drifted through her low-lit rooms,
Cats asleep on cupboards, a warm wood stove,
Frugal meals, bells outdoors and inside
Voices spinning yarns about village
Scandals and intrigues. My fantasies
Circled her pastures, climbing into the sky,
The myths she lived, death at the window . . .

And as the phone call became
Entrapped in the voice of the storm,
My grandmother animated the house,
Like the windy cliffs of some peak's clouds,
Like the fever chart of endless tomorrows —
Like a surrender
To some other edge of risk.

Moonlighting

When you flee to Italy
it improvises a classic
retreat with toasting friends
and a tang of privilege.
So the northern ethos gives over —
fortified faces to subversive wit,
potatoes and leeks to pasta and fruits,
misty forests to olive groves.
My Italy,
when it rises from the back stage of writing,
has only mountains, pilgrim poets,
our grandfather Rinaldo.
      It singles me out! *Simpleton*,
it calls, *stay away*.
The marketplace of nostalgia
holds few rewards.
Why moonlight with an Italy

if not to measure it against the true
home that governs us — our keepsake
we throw mindlessly from hand to hand,
its blessings dependable as clouds of rain.

DELIA DE SANTIS

Dinner for Three

"We should go out for dinner together — the three of us. To be civilized," he says.

I am in the kitchen and I have a knife in my hand. I picture myself placing the blade on one side of his face, just above his cheekbone, and slicing right into his apple round cheek. When I am done, I will hold the piece of flesh in my hand and look at it. It doesn't mean anything to me. It's a clean piece of flesh — not a trickle of blood to it. No mess at all. Who needs a messy mutilation?

I don't say anything and keep on working. I am cutting a squash into cubes. The skin is tough and I have to push really hard to get through it. But I don't mind; I have good strong wrists.

The palms of my hands are getting coated with the orange colour from the squash. I know that just soap and water will not take it off. I'll have to use bleach and it will make my skin feel tender and sore. But that doesn't matter . . . I could pour a can of acid on my hands and he wouldn't care. That's because he has her hands to think about. Those slender, young hands caressing his neck, drawing him to her . . .

I wonder what he thought the first time he kissed her. He must have forgotten I even existed.

"How does the Olde Country Steak House sound?"

"Homey," I say, smiling.

Now I can actually say I know the pain of smiling. Only a month ago, if someone would have talked about it, I would have been skeptical. I would have doubted there could be pain in smiling. No, I wouldn't have believed. But I believe now all right. It's as though I have taken a knife and cut a hole where my mouth is. Carved into my own flesh.

"Ruth," he says, shaking his head.

He wants to chide me for my sarcasm, but he knows it wouldn't do any good. Besides, he has no right to reproach me anymore. He's moving out tomorrow.

"Ruth," he says again, leaving the name hanging in the air like an object that can't be put down. I know that sounds weird. A name is not an object, let alone one that can hang in the air. But under the circumstances, I have a right to some insanity.

Yes, he's looking around for a place to let the name rest now. He can't stand to leave it suspended like that. It has to be placed somewhere. His head turns here and there. What about the top of the buffet? No, not there — not enough room. Too many pictures. Our four children and their spouses; thirteen grandchildren — our family.

"Nana, why are you getting a divorce?" five-year-old Megan asked me yesterday. I was at my daughter's house babysitting.

"Oh my little darling," I whisper, hugging the child so hard I nearly break her tender ribs.

"Why, Nana?" she asks again.

I make her sit on my lap. "You see, Megan . . . you're too young to understand."

She combs the top of my hair with her little fingers.

"Do *you* understand it?" she says, kissing my forehead over and over again.

I am not a person who cries easily, but yesterday I cried. And damn it, I am doing it again now. A tear has just fallen onto the back of my hand, but when he comes to stand beside me, the tear is not there anymore and I am glad. I avoid wiping my eyes so he won't notice anything. I have my pride.

"I'll make the reservations," he says. "Dinner for three. The Old Country Steak House. We'll talk. Be friends."

After he has spoken, he still doesn't move away. I don't want him close to me anymore. I associate his nearness with betrayal. We were walking together in the park when he first told me . . . the sleeves of our windbreakers touching . . .

"Listen," he says now, leaning toward me. "I still need your friendship. You know that, don't you?"

The squash is all cut up. I put it in a baking dish and cover it. There's still lots of time before supper — I'll use the microwave anyway and it'll be quick. I wash my hands, but I have decided not to use the bleach after all. I will let the orange colour wear off by itself.

After, I clean everything on the counter, leaving the knife till the end. I run cold water on the blade; I know hot water will dull a blade. I hate a knife that won't cut, that isn't nice and sharp.

The tap is running full blast. The blade gleams underneath the water . . .

"What are you doing, Ruth? What the hell . . ."

I pay no attention to him, but after a while I finally turn the water off. I wipe the knife and put it away. It takes me a minute longer than usual to close the drawer.

"For God's sake. Are you all right?"

Standing very still for a moment, I take a deep breath. Briefly, I glance his way. I never did like blood, and I am not foolish enough to believe that a wound wouldn't bleed. But I say nothing of this to him. What is the use.

Going to the closet, I get my coat. I am beginning to enjoy going for walks alone. This is the first time I have admitted this to myself. But from now on my life will be my own. I don't owe anyone anything. I certainly don't owe this man anymore than I have already given him. I trusted him . . .

"I guess I'll forget about the reservations," he says, holding the edge of the door. "You don't want to go, do you?"

I don't answer. I don't have to. I never said I would go. In fact, I didn't even hint I would. I am not ready to offer friendship. Maybe I never will be. The choice is mine.

It's autumn and everywhere the leaves are falling. I feel a little like a leaf myself . . . one newly detached from a branch. I am falling and I feel a little scared, but heady, too . . . the wind tossing me here and there before I land . . . the earth so soft this time of year.

The Colour Red

"They're moving in — next door," Alex said, looking out the side window.

Edith lifted her head briefly from her knitting. "Are they?"

"I just saw them unload the bed. It's one of these steel ones, with rails at the sides."

"You shouldn't let them see you watching, dear."

But he remained where he was. He shook his head. "I don't think he's doing the right thing . . . "

"It's no concern of ours," she said quietly. "If the man wants to look after his wife at home, he has every right to."

"The woman is senile, Edith . . . ."

"Alzheimer's — that's what it is." She had dropped a stitch and was trying to pick it up — she didn't usually drop stitches. "Anyway, some people are very dedicated to their loved ones."

"Well, there he goes right now. He looks so shabby — just the way the Millers described him. They were telling me the other day he wasn't like that before. He used to be smartly dressed all the time. Of course, he doesn't have any time for himself anymore. How could he, looking after her like that?"

Alex had always been meticulous about his appearance. A bit of mud splashed on the leg of his trousers could put a look of discomfort on his face; when his barber was away, Alex was so miserable you couldn't talk to him. And since his retirement two years ago, he had started to fuss even more about himself.

Edith was a soap and water person. Alex had always admired her for being practical about everything.

She saw the man next door for the first time the following day. She was working in the backyard when he opened the side door to let the dog out.

Barking loudly, the dog began running toward her. Edith drew back.

"He's harmless," the neighbour said. "It's the Doberman in him that scares people. But he won't bite."

She laughed, relaxing. The dog sniffed at her feet, and she patted his back.

"I'm Joe Lamont," the man said.

"Edith. Edith Stone."

"Nice tulips you have there. Hilda — my wife — she used to grow them, too. She hasn't been well for a couple of years now . . . She used to have them all along the front porch."

"I really like them," said Edith. "Last year I had to get all new bulbs, but if I look after them properly, these should be all right for a while. A person has to have *something*."

"That's true," he nodded. "Hilda used to have purple ones. She's always been fond of purple."

Edith looked down at her own tulips, planted in a circle. In the middle there were red ones, and on the outside, three rows of yellow. She couldn't say why she had picked those two colours. She had never thought about it before.

Joe Lamont had to go after his dog, to keep him from the road. She put her garden gloves back on.

Alex had lunch ready when she finished outside. They sat down at the table, but the soup was still too hot.

"I saw you talking to the new neighbour . . ."

"Yes, he came out with the dog."

"What did he say?"

"Oh, not much. He said the dog doesn't bite — I got a bit of a scare at first."

"Didn't he say anything about his wife?"

"He just said she hasn't been well. He didn't say what's wrong."

Alex shook his head. "He can't be taking care of her properly. It's impossible."

She lifted a spoonful of soup and held it for a moment before starting to eat. "He's probably doing all right. I'm sure that when he can't handle it anymore he'll look into the alternatives."

Alex noticed a loose button on his shirt and frowned. "Uh, what's he like?"

She looked up at him and didn't say anything for a long time. "Ordinary . . . a nice man."

He didn't want anything else after the soup and got up. She put some lettuce and a slice of ham on her plate, and watched him rotate his shoulders, trying to loosen up his muscles. He could build up more tension in himself than anybody else she knew.

When he went out in the afternoon, she thought it would be a good time to bake the pie. Usually she hummed while getting the apples ready, but today her mind just wasn't free.

After the pie had cooled enough, she went next door with it. She had made the same welcoming gesture with all the new neighbours.

"It's so kind of you," Joe Lamont said, pushing straggly grey hair off his face. "If you'd like to come in . . . but Hilda is asleep now. She dozes off a lot. It's from the medication . . ."

"No, it's all right," she explained. "I couldn't come in now anyway — I'm trying to get an afghan finished for our church bazaar."

"Edith," he said, pushing his hair back slowly this time, "I think I should tell you about Hilda's disease. She has Alzheimer's, you see. And sometimes she takes a liking to people . . . but sometimes she doesn't . . ."

"I understand," said Edith. "But if you ever need anything, you know where we are."

"Well, thank you so much." He took a whiff of the pie, lightly covered with aluminum foil. "I love the smell of cooked apples. We'll be having a nice dessert for a change," he grinned. "We're getting pretty tired of jello."

Back home, Edith sat down in the livingroom and picked up her knitting. Usually at this time of the afternoon she would turn the TV on, but today she didn't. As her needles clicked back and forth, she began to think about her husband's anxiety since the Lamonts had moved in next door.

After supper, she waited for the right moment to talk to him. "Dear," she began, "I did a lot of thinking today . . ."

"Oh. About what?"

"Well, we're not getting any younger, and I thought some things should be talked over. For example, if something should happen to me, like Hilda next door, I'd like you to know what to do."

"Now, now, Edith." Colour drained from his lean features.

"No, this is important, Alex. It will put our minds at ease." She paused for a moment. "I would like it better to be somewhere where there are other people with the same problem. You know — in a hospital or a nursing home."

Alex tried to conceal the relief he felt by assuming a cheerful tone. "Edith, you'll be just fine. Nothing like that will ever happen to you."

"No," she said, standing by the window, where she could see the tulips in full bloom. "I suppose not."

He came to put his arm around her.

She kept staring straight ahead. The circle of tulips became a blur, the colour red spreading like a slow — pouring wound onto the yellow.

Alex stroked her arm, slowly.

ANNA FOSCHI CIAMPOLINI

Interview with Antonino Mazza

Antonino Mazza has already published two English translations of works by Pierpaolo Pasolini: *The First Paradise, Odetta* . . . (from *Teorema*) in 1985, and *Alì Blue-Eyes And Other Prophecies* (from *Alì dagli occhi azzurri, Poesia in forma di rosa, La religione del mio tempo*, and *Teorema*). Mazza is the author of the poetry collection *The Way I Remember It* (Guernica, 1992), numerous essays and articles, as well as the experimental work of poetry in music entitled, *The Way I Remember it*, which he produced with the music of Aldo Mazza. He has also translated the complex collection of poetry *Ossi di Seppia*, by Eugenio Montale (*The Bones of Cuttlefish*, 1983).

In the winter of 1989, during one of his short visits to Vancouver, what had started as a relaxed conversation between two old friends was transformed into a riveting journey, a quest about the poetic and human essence of Pierpaolo Pasolini. Pasolini has been one of the most controversial figures in Italian literature, an author who, according to Alberto Moravia, "was simply the best poet we ever had during the second half of our century."

ANNA FOSCHI: Antonino, when did you start studying Pasolini's works?

ANTONINO MAZZA: Very late. I read very minor works and saw a couple of his films. I think it was 1982

when I began to read him seriously. I was in Rome with Eli
Mandell, who was teaching at the University. We took a
walk in the *English Cemetery,* a visit. Eli was interested in
the English poets. I had read *Le ceneri di Gramsci.* I didn't
find it very interesting, except in those poems where he was
not dealing with political themes. I abandoned him for a
time. Then, I came across "Alì dagli occhi azzurri," a
totally wonderfully disconnected work, and the poem *Pro-
fezia.* I suddenly realized that Pasolini had transformed
himself. In the beginning he was really afraid; he began to
liberate himself when he started to make films. He had a
huge perspective of what he wanted to criticize in society.
All of his early poetry is very classical. It was only when he
started to use the other medium, the films, that he realized
art does not have to be classical to be beautiful. He had an
incredible intellectual preparation, but he knew he had no
audience.

A.F. : Oh, I think he *had* an audience ... in those days,
in Italy, many people felt that reading Pasolini's works was
the highest form of intellectual snobbishness ... but, I must
say that our generation had only a superficial brush with
Pasolini's complexity. We, middle class people, could not
see the crisis he saw coming, in a society that, then, seemed
to offer so many promises.

A.M.: I went through his work to determine what his
time really was. Pasolini had a problem, he did not like
Histories. He had to negate present history, the move
towards a capitalistic society. Against that history, he had
to pose another history. His time was prehistoric. He felt
he was a member of the outside history. He was outside his

history and in time with pre-history. What happened in prehistoric times? They did not rely on memories but rather on oracles. Pasolini was projecting a pre-historic frame and inside that frame, the only thing that counted was not knowledge that came from the past, which is what counts for us. People then had to rely on sources of information that came from the future: the prophecy. He no longer relies on the past for enlightenment, for hope to go forward. Perhaps this all began subconsciously and he became aware of it later. He was tapping into intuition. He was totally preoccupied with the kind of knowledge, Cartesian knowledge, we rely on: we rely on the past. Let's consider, for instance, the rise of psychology during our time, a science that relies on the past. The metaphors he articulated, the sources he used were consistent with another cosmology, another ontology. This aspect of his, which is the most important, has not been looked upon seriously. He antagonizes the entire society, he threatens us all, he is totally radical. His words have oracular power. That is why he was hated. Even Moravia talks about his private life, his homosexuality. But these were minor transgressions, his major transgression was the subversion of time.

A.F.: But his private life was a subject that was constantly being discussed. It was an object of controversy, even of scorn. In those days, homosexuality was not easily accepted. In the eyes of *la gente*, the ordinary people, it cast a shadow even upon his stature as an artist.

A.M.: The other intellectuals stopped at the surface: "He's a pederast" because they felt threatened. Here is a man of his time and his culture, and he says this culture must be negated, and he creates the culture he negates. He could be either silenced or force others to negate it. He created a territory, a place which had no place, he imposed the margins he used as a measure of his freedom, the limits of the freedom that society imposes on its marginals: the women, the poor, the homosexuals and so on. He realized that the universe lives in the margin. The dominant culture *is* the margin, because it has to measure itself against the margin.

A.F.: Nevertheless, even Pasolini himself sometimes went back into "the margin." I remember, for example, his argument with journalist/writer Oriana Fallaci on certain aspects of feminism and on the matter of abortion . . .

A.M.: At the time, he had moved to a very dogmatic position against abortion. There are several letters by him, one article by her where she defends her feminist views. He is truly the voice that gave a large voice to post-modernism.

A.F.: Once more, Pasolini had chosen to be hated. I have to confess that I hated him too . . . I started to reconcile myself with him when I read one of his poems in *Il Corriere della sera*, during the times of the *contestazione* and of *gli anni di piombo*: *"i poliziotti sono figli di poveri"* [Cops come from poor families], he wrote, *" vi odio tutti"* [I hate you all], he said to the educated and affluent middle class, the bourgeois which posed as revolutionaries because it was the "in" thing to do. Then, I saw some of his movies.

A.M.: The films he made were archetypes of civilization: *Decameron, Arabian Nights, Edipo, Canterbury Tales,* and he re-interpreted them. He shattered their literary mould, so that anybody could get into it. In films, he took the classics and brought them back to the people. He was the first post-modern author in Italy.

He was a precursor, he wrote his poems in *Furlan,* not as a Furlan poet but as one who throws his book against the Italian language, one who says that the dialect is marginalized, and he wrote about aspects marginalized. The mixing of media is essentially a post-modern frame. The idea of contradicting himself . . . a very new concept.

A.F.: Do you think he lived his own "marginality," his being an outcast, a rebel, as an identification with "the marginal"?

A.M.: There are people who frame themselves according to the expectations of civilization. If you want to be a member of a society, you have to believe in its tenets, and you can become impassioned with them. But Pasolini had to come to terms with his passions, which were real passions.

An Interview with Mary di Michele

"Luckily, one day, my second-grade teacher brought our class to the public library: for five cents, I bought myself a library card and a whole universe." This is how Mary di Michele, the internationally renowned poet, remembers her first encounter with the world of literature. Since then, her unquenchable thirst for knowledge has brought her to explore a vast array of themes, whose inspiration takes root in the rich soil of the immigrant experience. Mary was six years old when her family left their home-town of Lanciano in the Abruzzi/Molise region of Italy and came to Ontario in 1954. Her first collection of poetry, *Bread and Chocolate*, speaks of aspirations and clashes between the ancient values of the peasant culture, treasured by the generation of immigrant parents, and the irresistible lure of the more independent, self-reliant existence that the North-American lifestyle offers to the children of immigrants. Soon, di Michele expanded her works to embrace other aspects of life: in *Necessary Sugar*, her poetic discourse analyzes the feminine condition, and that has always remained one of the most important streams of her poetry. In her interpretation of the complexity of women's position in life and society, she goes beyond the common stereotypes of feminism. There is no whining; no conventional self-pity. Instead, she pours into it the rare gift of a sharp intellect, of an imagery so intense and compelling which demands a sort of physical, visceral participation on the part of the reader. Hers is a lucid, disenchanted vision, which still vibrates deeply with authentic emotions. At thirty-nine, di Michele has established herself as one of the major poets in Canada and her works are well known in Europe and other countries. Her career is rich with achievements: in 1980, she won First Prize in the C.B.C.'s literary competition; 1982, the silver medal of the prestigious Du Maurier Poetry Prize. In 1983, there was the Air Canada's National First Prize.

Mary di Michele graduated from the University of Toronto, and her works are published in major literary magazines in Canada and the United States.

From poetry to prose: in the following interview, she talks about her first novel, *Voiceprints*. Once again, she returns to the theme of sexuality, to the subtle realm of sexual and spiritual bonds between man and woman, to their mysterious links with the cycles of human existence and of the human body.

Di Michele's personality is so rich, her civic and political stances are so extraordinary that this interview deals more with our world's social and political context rather than focusing on literary themes. It deals with her view of the ethical and moral dilemmas we are facing and will be facing in the future technological world we are creating. Di Michele's answers reflect her usual very unique and anti-conformist perspective.

ANNA FOSCHI: In your poetry, you speak about your immigrant roots, and of other universal themes: love, motherhood, the cycles of our life . . . where do you go from there?

MARY DI MICHELE: It's not so easy to explain the direction I am following now, or to talk about the projects I am working on right now. I am about to complete my first novel: *Voiceprints*. It's a feminist thriller exploring the dark side of contemporary sexual mores in North America, with an element of suspense. War in the bedroom! I am working on another collection of poetry, *Invitation to Darkness*. Many of the poems bear strong political connotations, they are based on real testimony, on true stories I heard during a visit to Chile last year. I am also thinking of writing a book of literary criticism. I have already written a paper for the Conference of Italian-Canadian Writers which took place in Toronto, last April. I felt quite a degree of personal involvement in writing that paper; I had the impression that I was barely touching the surface of the questions. I think that the set of problems of immigrants, or of the "colonized" people who write in a language which is not their own, who try to write in the *official language,* or in the language of the Empire, are very similar to the problems of women writers. Women writers write according to a *patri-archal* tradition, which excludes or marginalizes them. These writers are using strategies which are surprisingly similar. One of their principal strategies is the attempt to transfuse the physical body into the language. These are difficult questions, and I want to keep in mind the literary works being produced in the world, not just in Canada. The title of my first essay is: *Notes Towards a Reconstruction of Orpheus: The Language of Desire.*

A.F.: In our journey through the discovery of our own identity, we women went through many stages and many changes. We also contributed to profound changes in society. What can we still do in order to fulfill the promise of a world where a man and a woman can find a spiritual dimension which can be "immune to gravity"?

M.D.: We did not change society radically enough. In the Western world, women entered professions, the public sphere of the arts, but not the political sphere. They did not obtain political offices. In that way, all those men who feel threatened by the presence of women in other areas of public life, feel that they are safe, very safe in Parliament, or in Congress (depending on which country we are talking about). Certainly, at the Pentagon, they feel very shielded from any feminine influence. That explains the belligerent attitude of American politics. They want to prove that they are real *cowboys*. They are more afraid of being called "mama's boys" than they are afraid of communism. And that jeopardizes all the mutual promises that a man and a woman can exchange, no matter how loving and tender they can be.

A.F.: Today, the science of biogenetics is so advanced that scientists can intervene in the sphere of human reproduction and can interfere with the natural cycles of the female body. Do you think that for women, this means the liberation from Nature's ancient curses and burdens, or will it just become another "betrayal of ourselves caused by our species"?

M.D.: Let's take the science of biogenetics and let's bring it to an X level: then, are we going to need species and gender? And in what image are we going to be moulded? I think it's important that women start studying biogenetics, or we will end up in a world of *cowboys,* I suppose. I feel giddy!

Interview with Len Gasparini

" ... And, one beautiful morning ... indifferent as a beggar, to start my journey, walking until my legs wear down . . .

to die walking . . . ," Charles Lamb wrote in one of his letters. In English and American literature, since the nineteen century to the contemporary period, we find quite a number of "wandering poets." It was and it is the refusal of being conditioned by time constraints, by the demands of business, by social conventions, that inspired them. It was and it is the quest to re-discover, through the routes of the immense North American continent, the dimension of the eternal and of the sublime, just by travelling and going as far as they wish to go. They pursued their dreamy explorations by walking around, or galloping on a horse, and, more recently, by roaming around in huge cars, cars which are as big as ocean liners, and that Europeans perceived as the true icons of the nomadic spirit pervading the North American continent. Leonard Gasparini belongs in his own right to the strain of the "wandering poets," both in the literal sense and even more so in the metaphorical. His poetry speaks of a long spiritual journey, an itinerary which starts by looking at the human condition and ultimately leads to the contemplation of Nature. His works express an insatiable intellectual curiosity, an obstinate quest for the purity and clarity of the poetic expression, pursued by eliminating any superfluous element, until it reaches the absolute, conclusive simplicity of the children's rhymes, in some of his latest poems from *Ink from an Octopus.*

He was just passing through Vancouver, when I called him. On the phone, he balked, somewhat surprised, at my request for an interview for the series *Italian-Canadian Writers* : "Canadian? Italian? Perhaps, I would say,

American: I grew up in Detroit. Maybe, neither Canadian, nor Italian, nor American . . ."

But later on, enticed by a steaming bowl of *passatelli,* the Italian soup which is the *madeleine* equivalent of his not-so-forgotten Marchigiane roots, he recalled images and fragments of his adventurous childhood and adolescence, which were shaped by cultural duality. That duality later became imbedded in his poetic inspiration: "Through strange cities he passed alone,/doubting his own identity,/ discarding it piecemeal/ till he felt weightless, giddy" (from "Alter Ego"). He draws inspiration from the feeling of duality and from the unrelenting search for physical and inner freedom. This freedom has to be found in the continuous becoming, in the travelling as an existential experience that allows him to confront the essential and to "live" in the soul of Nature. Gasparini's poetry, especially in his latest works, is permeated by an intense rapport with Nature, a total fusion, whether he makes the glimpse of a landscape come alive with words, or pauses to observe the small living creatures: "The black and yellow striped caterpillar/ Munching on a milkweed leaf / Is a living metaphor, / A master of regal disguise / That can metamorphose itself / Before your unbelieving eyes (from "Monarch Butterfly"), and again: "To paint an octopus dying in the arms / of its own iridescence / was Walter Anderson's way of looking / into the eye of God (from "Homage to Walter Anderson").

Born in Windsor, Ontario, to a Trevigiana mother and a Marchigiano father, he grew up making frequent trips south of the border to nearby Detroit. He was a high school drop-out, because he was impatient to achieve his personal freedom. In order to do that, he worked at a variety of jobs. ("Even today, they call me the truck driver poet," he states.) At seventeen, he enlisted in the U.S. Navy. After that, he lived in Toronto and Vancouver, travelled to and resided in the United States and other countries, fathered four children and published a variety of poetry collections. Some of his works include *Moon Without Light* (published in 1978), *Breaking and Entering* (1980), *One Bullet Left* (1974), *I Was a Poet for the Mafia* (1974), and, in 1989, *Ink from an Octopus*. A one-act play, *Enough Rope,* was performed in Montreal in 1976. Recently, he has conducted extensive research on the life and works of American painter Walter Anderson. He is also researching on animism and Afro-Caribbean rituals, and is adding the finishing touches to his latest book of poetry, *Wild Garden.*

ANNA FOSCHI: Leonard, what is driving us to the perpetual quest for another reality?

LEONARD GASPARINI: When I was reading Dostoevsky, I became aware, for the first time, of the dualistic nature of the universe, in the literal sense. Dostoevsky revealed to me the intellectual significance, the intellectual experience of dualism, that before reading him, I could only perceive at an instinctive level.

By reading, I learned that everything is permeated by dualism: action/reaction, light/darkness, night/day, high tide/low tide. The roots of a tree burrow deep and find nourishment in darkness, but its leaves need light. To understand freedom, we have to experience the deprivation of freedom; freedom means many things, it has a literal meaning (we can talk about being free and being captive, for instance); but it has also infinite other meanings.

A.F.: Descending, from this cosmic dimension, to a human, finite one, how did this theme become part of your poetry?

L.G.: Partly, because I always liked reading, I always was an insatiable reader of poetry, of everything. My first experience with books was listening to my grandfather, who read *La Divina Commedia* every night. We lived together with our grandparents, who, even after years and years of living in Canada, had never learned to speak English. In the evening, my grandfather would sit in his rocking chair, with his tobacco snuff and read from that big book full of illustrations. It was my grandfather who taught me how to hold a pencil in my hand. Then, for a time, I was a semi-pro baseball player in Detroit; I had already received an offer to play with the Chicago Cubs when I finished school. Instead, I let go of baseball because I was too busy reading books, I was spending all my time at the school's library, I just wanted to experience new sensations. I have never been afraid of experimenting and sometimes I had to learn the hard way. My father never forgave me for not pursuing a career as a baseball player. But I found all my answers in the books.

A.F.: Did you feel the environment where you grew up was a bit repressive for you?

L.G.: I grew up in a neighborhood full of Italians, French and blacks. There were brawls everyday, as it happens with boys. At that age, the things that really mattered were sports and girls, the usual attractions of the adolescent years. Through reading, I realized that adventures could have a much greater dimension, an emotional dimension too, and that sparked my curiosity, my desire to explore things, places, feelings. Perhaps, I inherited all this from my father who read history books and books which dealt with Nature. My mother instead, lived a very traditional life, her entertainment was to go shopping and to go dancing. She was a good tango dancer; she used to go dancing at the Caboto Club with my Godfather, but she never acquired a driver's license, never learned how to drive a car.

A.F.: When did you publish your first poems?

L.G.: In 1967, when I was twenty-five. I did not have any literary models. As an adolescent, I admired Shelley, Keats. There were no Canadian authors I felt I had to follow in that sense, no writers I had to look upon. Layton was certainly an exception. Then, I was influenced, at the beginning of my career, by the American "beat generation," Gregory Corso, and that type of sub-culture, and among the Canadians, Irving Layton with his *A Red Carpet for the Sun* and Raymond Kinster. He was not a contemporary of Layton because he wrote in the 1920s and was somewhat alien to Canadian Literature. Canadian Literature has been influenced for so long by English poetry and fiction . . . and, as I said, I read American and British writers. When I began writing poetry, the subject matter, I would say, the predominant theme in my early poetry was sex. That, and a "tough guy" realism I tried to express. And, of course, that was also influenced by American films and

American literature, the early rock'n'roll music of the 1950s, Elvis Presley, jazz and the rhythm & blues. All of that contributed to a particular persona which I felt comfortable with and, I suppose, that obsessed me for a number of years, until I was stereotyped because I didn't have a very extensive academic background and I drove trucks for a living, and then I was labeled as a proletarian poet, the truck driver poet, which was O.K., because that's what I did. I married early, had two children, had a family to support. I was married at twenty-three, had to work, drive a truck. And gradually, the more I wrote, the more I began to publish. I was able at some point to conduct poetry workshops at local community colleges and do poetry readings. I also did a lot of readings of Canadian poetry. So I did readings at public libraries and schools all over Ontario. And then I got funding from the Canada Council and began to teach part-time, because I had been doing important workshops for years.

A.F.: And then, you started looking for new themes . . .

L.G.: Well, I wanted to understand as much about poetry as I possibly could, so I read, as I said earlier, American and British poets, European poets in translation, and Canadian poets. I became quite active on the literary scene for several years. I was very active in it, contributing to magazines, reviewing for newspapers and magazines, and reviewing books. I got into book reviewing because I enjoyed reading books. So I did a lot of reviewing for G. Woodcock, the editor of *Canadian Literature*.

But, as far as themes, the theme of experience was on my mind and still is, after the initial sensationalism of dealing with sexuality and poetry. I shouldn't say solely the sensationalism of it, but also its realistic aspect: the word *love* not only in its lyrical sense but often in its darker side, a kind of counterpart. I began to consider life both as a subject and as a voice for poetry and I tried to keep it chronological. Because, at one point, I was moving ahead, but I wasn't . . . My father, who read some of the works I had been doing, always suggested that I deal with aspects of Nature. Not that I wanted to ignore his suggestions, but I don't suppose I was ready yet. I was still unable to assimilate the natural world as well as he could. He wanted to make me see it, but it wasn't till 1983, after I read Rota and discovered the world of Walter Anderson that I began to see the natural world in a different light, so to speak. I was able to see it objectively, to understand it much more, and, since that time, it has been my quest, because Nature has its own metaphors; you don't have to provide metaphors for Nature. You receive metaphors from Nature, Nature gives you metaphors which are natural and that's where I am right now and will be until such time, you know . . . It is a process, you go through phases and ages, but, you know, you are growing and you are learning. I have been reading poetry for twenty years and I am still learning, still finding out things. I mean, because of the influences, when I began I wrote mostly in free verse, although I did extend that somewhat into rhyme and meter; with reference to free verse I think the influences were negative. So now I am more involved with form. There is no such thing as free verse, what's free about it? Verse is needed. So, with the work I am doing now, I am working with meter and rhyme and it's quite a pleasure working within the tradition rather than with the free verse, which can be a dead end.

A.F.: You told me that your last book, *Wild Garden,* is a children's book. But also some of your poems in *Ink from an Octopus* sound like children's rhymes in their apparent and subtle simplicity.

L.G.: Yes, in the third part of *Ink* . . . , in the poems about animals, there are all the indications for this new direction in my way of making poetry. But *Wild Garden* is a book for everybody, for adults, children, youth; it is a book to bring you closer to Nature, to make you aware of the world of Nature, of the things which are born and grow in a garden: insects, animals, grass.

All that without falling into the trap of anthropomorphism, which is the pathetic deception, the trite device used in so many works.

Instead, I read the works of writers who "live" Nature, like Edwin Way Teale, Jack Rudloe, W.H.Hudson. When I talk about Nature, that doesn't mean that I have jumped on the bandwagon of the ecological themes, which are so popular. It means, rather, that I feel like an observer, an instrument, it means that when I write I want to break free from the presence of the "ego." The beauty of Nature is often seen through the vision of the human "ego," through human subjectivity. I believe that, in order to see a tree, or a living creature, I must let my soul reach out to it. There is no human presence in Nature. I am distancing myself, in my poetic themes, from human and personal passions, which are always repeating themselves.

A.F.: Do you have any regrets, is there something you would rather not have done?

L.G.: It's better to stay away from regrets and self-pity. They are just useless. They stifle the emotional growth. Perhaps, I regret spending so many years in Toronto. For many years, I lived an urban existence, my first experiences happened in a urban environment. When I met Nature, that made spirituality tangible, gave a corporeal life to the spiritual quest through the observation, in the physical sense, in the mystical sense which enabled me to catch a glimpse of the supernatural within the natural. This is the point, the metaphysical is in the natural. And if we don't embrace what we see with our soul, then we cannot see anything, not an insect, not a grass blade.

Translated from the Italian by the author.

MARISA DE FRANCESCHI

The Race

We make love at the Hotel Diamond in San Marino. A fast and furious afternoon encounter that douses the flames of desire fanned by weeks of separation.

The once pristine sheets are now tangled and wrinkled. We lie back and smile contentedly at each another. Such passion still possible. It was times like these that made life tolerable, and sometimes wonderful, even if only for a few brief moments.

I watch Paul make a feeble attempt to extricate himself from the bed linen, then lie back exhausted.

I assure him he has every right to be tired. He smiles sheepishly, then closes his eyes. Despite the clatter beneath our window, he falls asleep almost instantly. The wandering minstrels, *contrada* bands and rhythmic marching don't reach him.

Even so, I pull the large French doors together to block some of the noise, then fling the flimsy curtains together to diffuse the light. The outside shutters I leave open so I can watch the medieval spectacle going on below and also keep an eye out for our son, Daniel, who should be coming up for a brief visit.

Daniel appears like a phantom from the future, like a star-trek character out-of-sync mingling with this time-capsuled crowd. Height alone makes him stand out. Why is it our American raised children are so much taller than their Italian counterparts?

I can see Daniel has been drained by the length of the trip. He is not at his physical best, and yet there is still an inexplicable aura of strength in his sleek yet powerful torso, his long but well massed legs. The locals look puny in comparison: the jester, thin and anorectic, the fellow beating incessantly on his small drum is a waif. The women too, although very elegant in their rich velvet medieval robes in deep purple, carob brown, burgundy or gold, with short trains sweeping the cobblestones, look diminutive and compact.

I smile at the incongruity. I rise from my perch at the window seat and wave down to Daniel. He nods his head and weaves through the circus below.

"What the hell?" he mutters as he climbs the stairs two at a time. "What's going on out there?"

"Medieval week in San Marino, son . . . You wouldn't believe it. The concierge gave me the lowdown: Nightly parades and marches as each *contrada* — you know, each quarter of the town — makes its way through the old part. Music from the period, archery, flag-throwing, you name it. And down there," I point to a nearby *al fresco* restaurant, "it's medieval fare: plebian soup, wild rabbit *papardelle,* stuffed lamb, wild forest mushrooms, and on it goes ad infinitum."

"On top of Worlds?" he says incredulously.

"Right on, son. I suppose they must figure World Championships come along once in a blue moon. Medieval week, on the other hand, is a yearly ritual."

"That's nuts."

"That's Italy . . . Oh, pardon me, That's San Marino. Have you noticed how insulted they are if you call them Italian?"

Daniel turns his head at the sound of his father's lionesque roar. "He's beat, isn't he?"

I nod. "Can you blame him?" I keep a straight face, not wanting Daniel to become suspicious of his father's most recent activities.

Daniel shakes his head. "Except for dinner, Dad stood all the way across. An eight hour flight. So I could have both his seat and mine to lie down."

"You're the Cyclist, son. You're the star."

In his usual manner, he abruptly changes the subject.

"Okay, so here it is. Everyone else has seen the course. They've been on it. Except *moi,* naturally."

I grind my teeth in agony. "I know. I know." Who could have predicted their plane would be grounded for technical problems and they'd have to wait twelve hours at the terminal for a replacement? All this before beginning the trans-Atlantic flight to Venice and then the long, tense drive to San Marino, liberally sprinkled with the usual traffic jams and accidents. Tourist season in Italy.

"So," Daniel continues, "The other guys have all been here at least a day and a night. I'm going to go out and take a look at the course. The team's having dinner at our hotel, a meeting, and hopefully, a good night's rest. Tomorrow we race." His eyebrows lift high and his eyes widen. He breathes out heavily several times, then coughs and goes into the bathroom to spit out phlegm.

"You're still sick, aren't you?" I ask.

"Don't worry about it," he calls as he forcefully runs water into the sink. He comes out wiping his face, now looking pale and drawn.

"Are you sure, son?" I ask.

"About what?" he replies nonchalantly pretending he doesn't know what I am referring to.

"The race. Are you sure you want to go through with it?"

"Mom, this is The Big One; World's."

That, for him, is the end of the conversation.

"See you tomorrow." He waves and makes a quick get-away.

თთ

Paul awakes just before sundown. I'd thrown open the French doors to let in the street sounds which had been escalating as evening drew near. Trumpets blared, drums pounded, each group with its own distinctive beat.

I smile and go over to kiss his sweating face. "Feel a bit better?" I ask. "If you hurry, we can watch the sun set behind those hills. Then we'll have the most wonderful dinner. Ottavio, the chef — he's the best in San Marino I've been informed, and . . ."

Paul cuts into my words as if he hasn't heard a thing. "Daniel?"

"He was here earlier." I force a smile — as much for myself as for him.

"How is he?"

"Looks better than you," I lie.

"Coughing?"

"A bit. But he says not to worry about it . . . Hurry," I tug at him. "We'll miss the sunset and the show in the Piazza." I want to postpone my own nagging worries, distracting myself with the on-going festivities. Paul's questions are keeping my wounds open.

He must sense my desperate attempts to forget about tomorrow's race because he changes the subject.

"You sure know how to pick them," he says glancing around at the room. "Must be a thousand years old."

"Actually, I think it's more than that," I joke. "It was all I could find. All of San Marino was booked."

"What's all that racket out there?"

"Long story. Come on. Let's go. You'll enjoy it."

"We won't see Daniel tonight?"

"No, he's checking out the course, then team stuff to do and you know . . ." I apply fresh lipstick and run my fingers through my hair. These are signals that I want to go out.

"I'm worried, Margaret. I'm worried about him. He was coughing up blood before we left."

"Blood?" That bit of news strikes me like a dagger.

"Yes."

"Did he take anything?"

"He can't. You know that."

I face Paul squarely and ask him bluntly. "If it were you, Paul. What would you do?"

He doesn't even have to think about the answer. It comes out naturally. "Race."

I nod my head. Why had I bothered to ask?

 හ

I've been in Italy several weeks. It's not something I told him or Paul, but I've lost the strength to watch Daniel race. I'd had my fill of crashes. My way out: arrange to go on ahead to San Marino, to find accommodations, to rent a car, to replace equipment misplaced or mangled in races leading up to The Big One: Hamilton Nationals: the body of an ergo power, cracked, causing brake levers to dangle uselessly, held only by a thin wire cable. An American race: a shattered tri-spoke sending pieces of styrofoam and carbon fiber flying through the air. Abitibi, Quebec: A badly cracked helmet after a fluke accident which tore through layers of spandex and gouged out large pieces of my son's flesh.

What better place than Italy for the Bottecchia parts, the Giro Helios helmet, I'd rationalized.

The clincher had been the tragedy in France where an Italian cyclist, riding with no helmet, had slammed into a concrete road marker and died instantly on the spot. Married with a child on the way. I'd only read about it in the papers, but that had been my breaking point.

I'd done all right, except for the Hotel Diamond. The site had looked magnificent in the brochure, and it was. Perched like a jewel, but in much need of buffing, it's former splendour was now tarnished and dull. It sits at the top of the hill in old San Marino, in the middle of the cauldron of events celebrating the yearly Medieval Festival. With World Championships here, who would have thought to ask if there would be other events going on? San Marino's sixty one square kilometers were saturated. I mean: fifty-five nations, fifty five teams, five or six on each team, plus the usual entourage of coaches and mechanics.

∞

Paul showers quickly. The water is lukewarm at best. I sit impatiently at the window seat and watch as swarms of costumed people press themselves into the piazza below. With them all together like this, the cacophony of sound from their instruments reminds me of symphony orchestra warm-ups. Paul rummages through his suitcase for clean clothes then joins me at the window. We have a clear view of the piazza which seems to be the meeting place. "Come," I say. "Let's try to find a spot over by the rampart." We lock our room door with a large iron key, then descend wide marble steps made slippery and worn in the centre by centuries of use. We push through the crowds and go over to lean on the stone wall. The cliff drops down several meters but not right to the bottom of the outcrop. Rolling hills wave like a green sea in the distance. The sun is a bright orange circle hanging in the sky above the hills. It looks like a picture a young child would paint. We watch the brilliant orb slip slowly down, as if melting right into the hills until finally all that is left of it is the rose tinted hue of the sky. "It was worth it, wasn't it, Paul?" I ask.

"That was remarkable," he admits.

᎐᎐᎐

Paul is up early. Nerves? His afternoon nap yesterday? Jet lag? I feel his eyes on me. They are burning through my thin skin. I don't want to face this day. I want to miss it entirely, wake up tomorrow when it will all be over. But I open my eyes.

"I want to take a look at the course," he says kissing my forehead softly. "You don't have to come."

But, of course, I go with him.

᎐᎐᎐

In the feeble early morning light, the town of San Marino seems even higher than its seven hundred fifty meters. I look down, but a dense fog lies like a mantle at the mountain's feet camouflaging the bottom. The sight is eerie. A haze has settled higher up on the rocky outcrop and higher yet, clouds threaten.

"Rain?" I ask.

"They said it wouldn't. It's early, Margaret. It'll all dissipate as the day goes on."

We walk down to one of the parking lots, the only places in the old town where vehicles are allowed to be stationed. The loud echoes of our footsteps are thrown back at us by the ancient walls. We jump into our rented Alpha Romeo and I unfold the race course map: 11.2 Kilometers, ten switchbacks at least, twenty-three turns, climbs that give a whole new meaning to breath-taking, thigh crunching 13% grades. And it all has to be done eleven times.

౪

The rain starts with innocent spurts up on the higher elevations. Then, as we coast down and wind through treacherous turns, there are patches of dry road. Not a good omen. Bales of hay have been tied protectively to concrete light posts and other potentially dangerous perils: the corners of buildings close to the road, monuments, statues, ancient fountains. At one downhill hairpin turn, three bed mattresses have been anchored to tree trunks — the only things between the riders and the cliff.

"I don't want to see this," I tell Paul. "Take me back to the hotel."

౪

The rain is coming down in earnest now. The slick roads would be treacherous.

Two-hundred and sixty-eight riders wait on the Via Napoleone Buonaparte for the ready signal. Paul and I are nowhere near the start/finish. Somewhere in the midst of that mass of colours, our son is revving up for the race.

౪

I don't look at the television monitor which is only meters away from where I stand. I don't look until I hear the commentator's voice raise frantically. "A crash," he roars in

Italian. "A spectacular crash . . . Right at the start/finish, ladies and gentlemen. Incredible. Absolutely incredible."

I hear no more as I turn my head towards the television screen to see dozens of riders fall like dominos, metal crunching, wheels squealing, thumps and thuds. I stare, mesmerized, my eyes spilling tears of fright, my lips quivering, my body shaking. "No," I cry. "Please, God, No."

And then, there, miraculously, I watch a small group of riders make their way through the centre of the mass of flesh and metal that has somehow managed to fall to either side of the roadway leaving just enough room for the lucky ones to sneak through. Like the dead sea parting. In a flash, I see Daniel.

I look about feverishly for Paul. Where is he? Where did he say he would be? Has he seen this? But there is no time to go looking for him now. The racers who survive the crash are already on the Strada Sottomontana, the straightaway where I have stationed myself knowing this was one place Daniel might try a breakaway at some point later in the race.

Daniel speeds by me. His sleek body seems molded to the frame of his bicycle. His knees tight, his head low, elbows in — he and the bike are one.

I snap my head to follow my son with my eyes. In a few lightning-fast seconds, he is a blur. I squint, hoping for another glimpse, instead I spot Paul who is running madly towards me.

I too begin to run. "He's okay," I shout. "He was in the pack. Didn't you see him?"

"No. No. I didn't. There was a crash. At the start/finish."

"He went through. He's okay."

"Are you sure?"

"Yes, Yes. I saw him. He just went by."

"I'll go back to that damned turn down there," he shouts breathlessly. "Someone stole two of the mattresses."

"What?"

"Two. Can you believe it? Sometime this morning. I'm going to stay there."

In the heat of the moment, I hadn't noticed the sun attempting to streak through the clouds. "Holy Jesus, thank you," I say lifting my eyes towards the heavens. But out beyond San Marino, hovering above the not too distant hills, more clouds seem bent on rolling in.

∞

The sudden downpour is responsible for other crashes. I can no longer watch the television monitor nor listen to the commentator who is explaining how the rain has decimated the riders. All I can do is watch for the red white and blue jersey.

When the main pack speeds by once again, he isn't there. My heart stops. It is lead in my chest. Why, I ask myself? Why do they do this? What is it they want? Have they no fear? Why? Why? Why? My question wants to scream out but I hold it inside where, unseen and invisible, it explodes ripping and shredding my heart.

༄

I spot Daniel. His face is covered with bright red blood. It rolls off his face and onto his jersey mingling with all the colours there, creating new patterns on his team uniform. I run out to him, only to be forcibly pulled back. "No, *signora,*" the man warns. "You can't go out on the race course."

"But it's my son," I cry.

He holds me tightly as I struggle for freedom. I watch Daniel brush blood from his face. Finally, he sees me and nearly collapses into my arms.

"See, *signora,*" the man says. "He knows when to stop."

༄

"Mom," Daniel says, shaking me as if I am the injured party. "It's okay. Just blood. From my nose. And my throat, I think. Not a crash."

I smile. "Is that supposed to make me feel better?" I ask.

༄

Only a quarter of the riders complete the race. The Podium was all red, white, and green: Italian. So much for my theory on bigger means better, I say to Paul later.

"I'm not too sure you should give up on your theory yet," he snickers. "I hear the Italians have been here for weeks. And they haven't been sight seeing."

"An unfair advantage, you're suggesting?"

He just shrugs his shoulders. "It's part of the game. No use complaining."

"But it's over, darling," I add. "It's finally over."

"Thank God," he whispers.

"They're all going down to Rimini tonight. To celebrate. To the discos. The Americans, the Russians, the Italians. I wouldn't want to be in Rimini tonight," I smile.

"He looked good after he cleaned up all the blood, didn't he?" Paul asks wanting to be reassured.

"Yeah, he did. I don't know why, but he did. Relieved, maybe."

Paul nods in agreement.

∞

Tonight is the final evening of the Medieval festivities. The highlight: the Cross-bow competition. Ancient rivals from all segments of San Marino and from such far away towns as Gubbio, Urbino, Ferrara, Arezzo will be competing for the honour of being this year's victors.

The rhythmic beating starts in the early evening, escalating as each *contrada* weaves through the ancient streets, past the Hotel Diamond and down to the very edge of a cliff at the far end of town. We watch from our front row window seats as spectators follow sheepishly procession-like. Paul and I finally go out and join them.

"Where on earth did all the people come from?" he asks amazed.

I shrug my shoulders. I find it as amazing as he does. Bread and circuses, I think. Keep the populace under control by giving them just the right amount to satiate their appetite for spectacle. Let them vent their frustrations watching dangerous and sometimes gory dramas. Is this not what the Romans had done? Gladiators torn apart by animals in structurally magnificent amphitheaters, mock naval battles in a piazza flooded for the occasion, horse racing in a tiny town square. All blood curdling sports. The Romans, those masters of architecture, who had home heating and indoor plumbing two thousand years ago, also loved blood and gore.

I add cycling to the list of dangerous spectator sports. So, how far have we come from Roman times, I wonder?

Paul pulls me away from my morbid thoughts and back to the present. "Margaret," he says putting a hand on my shoulder, "It's a sea of people. Look around."

The alley ways, barely wide enough to hold four abreast, are rivulets of people — each and every one following the procession to the cross-bow pit — a deep amphitheatre cut out of the rock, walls seven or eight meters high. At one end of the pit, stone steps accommodate those who first enter the arena. Ring side seats. They could keep them. Those cross bows looked deadly. At the other end, set upon a wall of stone, the target.

A contestant would no sooner draw his bow when a loud thud would be heard in the target area. Try as I might, my eye can not detect the dart that flies invisibly across the amphitheatre. Bulls-eye. Someone has hit it. A San Marinese. Squeals of joy permeate the night.

๛

Ottavio brings us his finest champagne with a late night snack of fresh bread, cheese, olives, marinated mushrooms and a few delicate pastries.

"*Tuo figlio?*" he asks. "Okay?"

"*Sì, sì,*" we assure him. He's okay.

"*Mi dispiace,*" he tells us.

"It's okay," we assure him. "He can't win them all. Besides, your Italians won everything. You should be proud."

"Ah," he corrects us. "*Io sono San Marinese.*"

"Right," we excuse ourselves. You're not Italian."

๛

The night is a silky silence. We sit on the large bed and sip our champagne and watch the curtains billow gently in the warm breeze. It could be the wine, or the release of tension, but we find ourselves in each other's arms.

"Repeat performance?" Paul asks.

๛

At three in the morning, the familiar sound of bicycle spokes tuning splits the quiet night. I get up quickly to watch my son pedal up the steep hill to the Hotel Diamond. He'd agreed to sleep at our hotel tonight so that we can get an early start in the morning. We've managed to convince him to scratch the German races from his itinerary. We're going to go north to the Alps where he can do some hill training, but also find time to relax.

"I'll come down and open the *portone,*" I whisper to Daniel. "Ottavio gave me the key."

Paul awakens when Daniel enters the room. He gets up and takes the bike from him, caressing it. "Get some rest, son," he says giving Daniel a fatherly pat on the shoulder.

Daniel flops on the bed which Ottavio has brought in for us. It is along the wall, next to his father's side of the big bed. Daniel turns towards his father.

"Dad," he calls.

"Son?"

"There's always next year."

ൟ

And the year after that, and the year after that, I groan inwardly, knowing this is just a temporary reprieve. Soon it will all start over again.

ISABELLA COLALILLO-KATZ

The Sound of a Distant Wailing

for A.C.

I

Parts of my childhood
fall away
in a slow reel of backwards
images
unwinding
to a final scene
as each old relative
is touched
and moves
reluctantly
into death's watchful shadow,
disappearing
from the very photographs
we kept
in dusty closets
taking them out
from time to time
to remember
the way we were
and looked

and laughed
in other times and places.
    The faces of the dead ones dim
in the photograph album
surrounded by old documents,
faded papers
attesting to our acts of transition
from there
to here
to now
where we find ourselves
once again
burying our dead.

II

    To her I give back these memories:
to this stubborn aunt
who moved undaunted
through three continents,
always courageous
always smiling.
    Her small, stout body and
fine cropped hair
deep, grey eyes,
trailing a wistful smile in
a mix of Italian dialect
and the Buenos Aires Castellan
from her years
in Argentina
where alone,

she raised two children
after her husband's
slow death:
his polluted lungs
bringing him to final silence.

    For years she sat
alone
on a small, rough bench
in a suburban Toronto garden,
fragrant with flowering pear trees,
watching for early roses
as she rested from her work.
    She raised three Canadian
grandchildren
with no English.
With easy love she taught
them hybrid latinate sounds,
tolerating their harsh shaped
saxon words
at the dinner hour,
understanding little of their chatter.

    In our scattered family
she was an elder,
one of the few remaining.
In her last years
as fragile as a lonely twig,
whose stubborn leaves
are wooded away

by the whispering
promise of hurrying winds.
    And one day,
like a withered oak leaf
she fell
on the stone hard April ground
never again to return
to the warm spring garden.

III

    The graves at Holy Cross
are filling up. Rows
and rows of resting places
neat and well kept
at the edge of a foreign city.
    From here the hapless dead
look down to the merciless city
that took their dreams,
used up their memories
ate up their lives like bitter bread
to the moment of final breath.
    This is the last port
holding a thousand immigrant bones;
yet no visible sign remains
of their tired days and struggles.

    In neat rows and depths,
they lie in solitary arrangements:
friends, family and neighbours
in permanent sleep.

It's hard to find
an uncle or a cousin
whose bones lie weary,
unless someone
more familiar with the place
points to the spot.
Then you watch the flower vases
appear from their hiding place
turning up empty and bronze
and you wish you'd brought
some flowers.

IV

It is April again.
The sky fills up with lark songs.
The day is cloudless and dry
as we follow the coffin.
Zia is finally buried,
in a grand mausoleum
(a gift from her grieving children),
never again to return,
to the dulling sounds of the garish city,
where our brief lives survive
like short spring blooms.
Another funeral is done.
There have been three or four this year,
all members of our family
and not all old —
just weary and empty of light.

Today
another funeral moves
among the graves
in a quiet shuffling of tears;
muffled wails
and knots of black bandannas
shadow the sallow, solemn faces
of dark eyed, weeping women
holding prayer beads
in work worn hands;
their Sunday shoes
like worn slippers
on the slippery new grass.
    The burden of pain
borne by the silent men
walking in sober pairs
holds up a sheet of silence
against secret tears.

    The dead do not awaken
to the soft crying
and the murmur of ancient prayers.
Even when the living mumble their names
in old dialects, the dead say nothing.
It is the living who remember
the countless voyages,
laced with the tears of constant partings:
the endless journeys from homeland to place.
The dead no longer hear the slow
and slender syllables bound by

sorrow and hope.

V

    Larks are circling overhead.
Soundless wingbeats stir
in the trundled air.
Worms burrow inward
tearing the earth's deep flesh.
In this place of frozen dreams,
far from their village homes,
the mourning, doleful song
of wailing, black robed women
chanting death's unwelcome
coming
is quietly remembered.

    The silence is remarkable.
It reminds me of the crucifixion scene
in Pasolini's *Gospel*
According to St. Matthew
where the absence of sound
amplifies
the black and white imagery
making the point of death's lament
more poignant
in the gaping throats of the living.

    Here, in this place —
in this flat Canadian meadow —
the wailing sound of southern rural towns

seems absent.
It lies inside them
in the dead and in the living
like a lost dream.

VI

On an ordinary Saturday in April
the hushed Canadian ritual
is played out
new and unformed
like the unborn rites
of a lost tribe.
The quiet shuffle of bedroom slippers
trembles
against the crackling sound
of a rogue wind,
fingering stiff black clothes.
Again the image unfolds
in a filmy glaze
over the soundless landscape.
Two crows observe the movement
as the one legged woman
who was our aunt and mother,
grandmother,
sister and friend
is laid to final rest
in the curve of this wild green land
she never really knew.
Alive only
in our memories

and fading photographs.

To the crow's curious eyes
the scene unfolds,
in a soundless image
under a vast blue sky.
And in the depth of this photograph
in this teeming moment of utter stillness
through the soundless, eyeless years
I hear
the faraway sound,
the persistent,
echoing cry,
swelling and
immutable,
the sound
of a distant
wailing.

My Mother's Poem

She leans into her pain
closer and closer to its
clawing blindness —
a growing darkness
on a wide starry plain.

She picks up her pen
and stabs at the face of pain
grown long horned
and hungry
over long years.
Among the waves of thoughts
washing up
on the shores of her life,
she collects
wounding images,
glinting swords
piercing her days and nights.

She writes
in the old dialect,
stringing words
like rare jade
on a strong white thread.
Her memories a relief,
a fresh breath
shaping the theme of her poem:
her lost youth
her violent removal from the womb
of her mountains after the war
the loss of her people
their shared language
and lost dreams.

I can barely make out her
writing —
she has written in some
kind of shorthand —
so she reads it out loud,
the pasta cooking in the
Sunday pot
is boiling
over.

As she reads,
the words form
in the ears of my first language:
village smells rise up
into forgotten sounds
vespers chiming
against the trill of croaking frogs
old kitchen voices
crackling stories around the winter fire
and the dusty roads we walked together
me holding her hand
so long ago.

Her heart become a lava
pouring out quiet words
against the sobbing October rain.
The old dialect
bubbles in my soul
like an untasted
vegetable.

Aching sounds beat
against my heart
opening up channels of words.
I want to say,
"I like it.
You are a fine poet."
But the praise won't come.

She closes her notebook
and returns to the Sunday cooking
stirring silence
into food.

I stand mute,
suspended in
the spell of haunting
images, clutching
her green notebook.

My mother's poem
churning
through my fingers
like an ancient rain.

CATERINA EDWARDS

The Lion's Mouth

IX

The first time I tried to write of you I was fifteen. The summer before I had fallen in love with you. Do you remember? You happened to be broke, between jobs, between girls, so you spent much more time with me than you ever did before or again. "*Bambinona*," you called me. Big baby. I almost didn't mind. Your voice was so gentle, so intimate when you said it. Besides, I was grateful. Riding the *motoscafo* to the Lido, then the bus to the cheapest beach — hour upon hour of talking. Lying in the sun, eating at cafés, sitting in your room watching you play your guitar. Hours upon hours. *Bambinona*. But you were the first man who attended to me, who let me tell.

In that first attempt at a novel, though, your role was preeminently symbolic. My main concern was in telling the story of 'a sensitive Italian girl' who emigrated, with her parents, to the prairies, who emigrated to loneliness and isolation, more, to an eventual mental and physical decay. For she was destroyed by the hostile, cold land. There was much dwelling, with no sense of contradiction, both on the emptiness, the ghostlessness and on the hostility, the cruelty of the prairie. I was to discover much later that all my personal, deeply felt comments, "the cruelness of a straight line," "the monstrous mountains," were the commonest of clichés. I had never read a Canadian book, yet I reproduced not only themes but images, lines.

You — Gianni was the name I gave you — represented Venice lost. Gianni was also an immigrant, a fellow "sensitive soul," but one who retained, more, promoted gentle memories, old customs and habits. Still, Gianni refused to save my doomed heroine, leaving her and the wastes for Europe and a new, brilliant career as an opera singer.

Rereading that first attempt is embarrassing. I don't like being reminded of my adolescent, histrionic self. So tedious! But, sigh, we must own what we were as well as what we are. Besides, it illuminates the depth of the shock my family's emigration from Venice to Canada caused. For my life was split into two seemingly inimical halves, not only between the time before and after, but through all my growing years: Italy in summer, Canada in winter. Italy was enclosure, cocooning, the comfort of a secure place among the cousins, aunts, uncles, grandparents. There was always a surfeit of noise, of concern, of advice — of hands straightening the bow in my hair, grabbing me for a hug. A surfeit of regulations: "You can't drink that, it's much too cold; you can't go out alone; you can't wear that dress; you can't, you can't. It's not *done*." A surfeit of voices bouncing through the vague dark of those rooms shuttered against the summer sun and heat. Maybe because I was the youngest, you all turned me into the family pet; a doll to be dressed and decorated. My jewelry box is still stuffed with tiny gold chains, bracelets, rings. It was part of your childhood too — that closeness, carefulness, the insulating blanket of protectiveness, all springing from a hysterical perception of outside. Danger lurking at every corner, glowing from every strange eye.

Leaving Venice for the first time, I confronted ten days crossing the ocean, ten days staring at the limitless waves, three even more endless days on the train. Rock and tree, tree and rock. No houses, no people for hundreds upon hundreds of miles. The villages and towns where the train did stop seemed ill-proportioned, perched upon the land rather than rising from it. The only change came in the giving way to prairie — a land to my untrained eye still more monotone, still more desolate. Leaving Venice, though I was with Mamma and Papa, I felt stripped of family, of friends, of familiar walls and buildings, of proper landscape. I was exposed, alone in the nothingness.

XII

Marco closed and bolted the front door. He carefully checked room after room to be sure that everything was in its proper place. He started *The Four Seasons* on the record player. Then, and only then, as he sank into the sofa and those first notes rang out triumphant, was he overcome with relief. They were gone. He was alone with no duties until Paola and Francesco arrived at Piazzale Roma. He put his slippered feet on the coffee table. He didn't even have to get dressed. He would listen to records, as loud as he wanted, sketch a bit. If he could concentrate. If he could draw anything besides the line of Elena's shoulder, the curve of her bare arm (when she ruffled her hair), the compact roundness of her breasts. She was a broad, heavy rock damming up the free flow of his mind. It was so tidy her turning up when she had, the one night when Paola was away. But how could their meeting in that café not have been accidental? How could she have known? Had one of her little band designed some wondrous machine, a type of divining rod, that sought out vulnerability? Beep, it had gone when he had happened to cross its path — beep, beep — identification: moving target. No, perhaps sitting duck was the appropriate tag: sitting, waiting, unaware, unable.

The phone rang.

"I hope you're not planning to go out in this. And Francesco? Will Paola have enough sense? It's terrible, terrible; the water's coming through the bottom of the door. Every year it's worse." His mother spoke so quickly that the words seemed to knock into and fall over each other like tin soldiers.

"Do you need help?"

"Aren't you listening? You stay home. I've moved everything. I tried to call Tarquinio, but his phone was busy. Who could he be talking to for so long? It must be Lea. You know her, loves to gossip. Or Patrizia, though it does seem a bit early in the morning for her."

"I must ask you a favour."

"The siren was only four bells, so it should stop soon. Start going down. I hope. I don't understand it — it's January, not November."

"Mamma."

"What do you want?"

"I had to lend out some wading boots and I'm going to tell Paola that I lent them to you. Do you understand?"

"I'm not stupid. You want me to lie."

"I doubt she'll even mention it, but just in case. You dropped in this morning. The boots you had weren't adequate. You can think of something, I'm sure."

"Who did you lend them to? That divorcee who lives in the apartment above yours? You always did have a weakness for blondes."

"Yes, I did actually. But don't get me wrong. She was stuck. And you know how Paola is. I thought it would be easier . . ."

"I always knew that blonde was out for what she could get. You let people get familiar too easily. You should be careful."

"Mamma."

"Don't worry. I wouldn't give Paola any other reason to sink her fangs into you."

"I have to go."

"Someone's there?"

"The coffee's probably boiling over."

"I should come over, make you a nice lunch. A little broth, a soft coddled egg."

"And the water? Besides, I have work to do."

"You have to eat."

"Tarquinio said I can drop in there if I want."

"They didn't say anything to me. It's your Aunt Elsa; she's always been against me. Even last night, after you left. I was trying to reason with Patrizia about the makeup and the boy she's been seeing — her mother's heartbroken, you know — the way she carries on; it's inevitable, she'll come to a bad end, just you wait and see. Anyway, Elsa started in on me. Telling me that it was none of my business and that I was making it worse. As if she knew; she doesn't know what it means to be a mother. So now, I said, *now* I'm not even allowed to speak —"

"I can smell the coffee burning. Must go. Call me if you need any help."

Marco put the needle arm back to the beginning of the record, turned the volume up and settled back on the sofa. He wished he still smoked, not from any bodily urge for a cigarette but because it seemed an appropriate accompaniment to his state of mind. Perhaps he should go and put on some more coffee. But before he could rouse himself, the music began to play on him.

Once, on a Sunday walk, when Paola had been pregnant with Francesco, they had found the Piazza emptied, all the people confined by police to the sides, in preparation for a historical parade, part of the celebration of the Regatta of the Four Maritime Republics. The square, unobscured by the usual crowds, was exposed in all its beauty. "The living room of Europe." Two thousand years of history: Greek, Byzantine, Gothic, Baroque, coexisting in harmonious balance, a melody of man's potential.

Then, as if giving voice to the emotions of the viewers, over the loudspeakers attached to the church came the first notes of 'Autumn' from *The Four Seasons*. The pigeons scattered over the square, in unison flew to a central spot and, as a flock, flew back and forth across the Piazza and

Piazzetta controlled by the rhythm of the music. Paola took his hand and pressed it to her belly where he could feel their child kicking out as if it too could hear and respond to the glorious notes. The pigeons flew gradually higher, a grey blur before the glittering church, the gold-encrusted clock, higher into the deep blue May sky, interweaving by their flight the songs of the square, the music, the child-to-be into an almost heavenly cantata of human possibility.

The phone rang again.

"It took you a long time to answer." Paola's voice wasn't quite as neutral this time. He could hear the slight hysterical edge.

"I was in the *salotto* listening to music."

"How nice."

"You didn't sleep?"

"Some. I took a pill. But I still tossed and turned."

"I should have been there . . . And Francesco?"

"He seems all right. The other specialist is with him now."

"They haven't told you anything?"

"Not much. But I think it's worse than we thought."

The cold-eyed men. Merciless. "No, not worse. I knew . . ."

Her voice cracked ever so slightly. "You always know — don't you?"

"Paola." Silence. "When are you coming home? We can discuss it properly then."

"I was going to take the 2:05 train, but I heard the water's high. We can't expose Francesco to . . ."

"It's not too serious. You can call just before you leave, see how it is. I could always bring boots to the station. We could get a taxi."

"Don't you understand? We can't take risks."

"And I'm saying there'll be no risk. Look, if you don't come home, I'll come to Padova."

"I'll call you." And, in a very Paola-like move, she hung up.

"Worse than we thought." He *had* known, known that the white-masked men could only find the worst. Their rubber-gloved hands probed for the flaws in the machine. And in a child who was essentially flawed?

Poor Francesco. A hole in the heart. Ironic since if anything he was "all heart." Jammed full of indiscriminate affection. *"Bacini, bacini,"* kisses, kisses, was his most frequent phrase.

It had taken Marco and Paola six months before they had conquered their bitterness enough to have Francesco baptized. Before the service began, with the whole family standing around the baptismal font, Padre Lino had taken a sleeping Francesco from Paola. He had held him, smoothing down the voluminous skirts of the lace-embroidered baptismal gown. "I have thought much about this child and children like him. But only recently have I seen that the birth of Francesco is a cause for rejoicing. For God has sent you a saint. This child will never know sin. What more could a Christian parent want?"

"Everything," Marco had wanted to shout. But, of course, he hadn't. The service had gone on. Marco and Paola had renounced the devil and declared their belief in "the forgiveness of sins and the resurrection of the body" on Francesco's behalf. Certain things were not done. Oh, Marco would have liked to have accepted this salve for the wound, but he had been without belief for so long. Still, now, after watching Francesco grow, after hearing his laughter, seeing his eagerness to please, to love, he understood what Padre Lino had meant. Blessed are the innocent. And the doctors, they did not judge the value of simplicity of heart. No. Their judgements were based on genetic codes. "If only we'd tested when Mrs. Bolcato was pregnant, one of them had said, "we could have arranged for her to go to London for an abortion. No problem at all."

The phone rang like an alarm. His body contracted in surprise. His hand was still resting on the receiver. *"Pronto."* Marco could hear a blended roar, trucks, cars, and people, but no answering voice. *"Pronto."*

Finally, just as he was about to hang up. "Marco?"

"Yes. Who is this?"

"Your overnight guest." It was Piero, but his voice seemed distorted both by background noise and by nervousness.

"Yes."

"A message must be carried to a friend. It's very important."

"I'm sorry but I'm very busy. My son is coming home and . . ."

"I realize that but this must be done."

"Not by me."

"Look," Piero's voice went slightly higher in register. "Your wife has had enough to deal with these last few days.

It would be unfortunate to agitate her further with more disappointments."

"What are you getting at?"

"Listen. I have a letter here with certain information . . ."

"She won't believe you."

"Certain details, a mention of a certain arrangement of objects in your bedroom to show that the writer . . . and there are the boots."

"This is despicable."

"No," he raised his voice a bit to be heard over the growing background din. "Just a necessity."

"How long will this go on?"

"This is the only time. Once the message is carried, I'll destroy the letter. You have my word."

"Not very reassuring. Why should I believe you?"

"There is no other way." But Piero's voice had an uncertain note to it. "Now listen carefully, we're running out of time. Go to the Bellini room at the *Academia*, at 11:30 this morning. There'll be a young man in a black coat and a red plaid shirt. Begin talking to him about one of the pictures. Then, casually, you must say to him, 'This is a time of action.' If he answers 'a time of terrible beauty,' tell him, 'if the water is down, the demonstration begins at 16:00.'"

"That's all?"

"Yes. Everything clear?" Marco repeated the instructions and the message.

"But nothing's clear. I didn't agree to . . ."

"The agreement was made last night." And Piero, like Paola before him, had hung up, leaving Marco with his mouth open, words shrivelling in the back of his throat.

XV

The galleries were empty. Room after room unfolded themselves to him — his private preserve. Even when he came to see a particular picture, he would meander, pause at a few favourites — Giorgione's *Tempesta*, Carpaccio's St. Ursula series. But this unlikely morning, when each painting seemed to hang for his eyes, he could not stop. The message he was to deliver, the words he must utter, shimmered in an insulating haze around him. His steps were soundless on the grey carpet, but his way was high-lighted by the skylights and the track lamps against the blur of the pictures.

As he approached the early Renaissance rooms, he found a covey of Australian tourists. Their faces were turned to the paintings, but they were loudly congratulating themselves on their intrepidness and cleverness in having found the gallery open. Marco edged past — they were half-blocking the doorway — into the long room where he knew a few of the Bellinis to be. Giovanni Bellini. Was this the gallery? There was *Sacred Conversations*, the colours glowing at him. But could this be called the Bellini room? Had Piero even meant Giovanni, or was it Jacopo or Gentile? How would it be judged if he missed the man? Would "I wasn't sure where you meant" serve? Quiet. Piero would not be random in his choice. There must be a thread of reasons, however fine. Sacred Conversations. No, that implied a delicate irony inimical to Piero's style. It must be something by Gentile, that acute observer of external rather than spiritual realities. The Bellini room. Of course, Room XX, the paintings commissioned by the School of St. John the Evangelist. Only two of the three paintings were by Gentile, but that still made it more of a Bellini room than where he was, which had three Giovanni's out of twenty.

And, in fact, when he reached Room XX, he realized that from a practical — never mind a symbolical — point of view, this must be the designated meeting place. It was off the main tour path and small in comparison to most of the galleries. Sitting on the bench, Marco could see both doorways, yet seemed to be intent on observing those tremendous paintings.

Eleven twenty-seven. At least he was at the correct place at the correct time. He leaned back, clasped his hands around his knees and let his eyes focus on the Bellinis. In the first, *The Procession of the True Cross*, he saw only the glowing gold, the touches of red, the balance and symmetry of the figures, but when he shifted to *The Miracle of the True Cross,* the size, the intensity, the vitality of the picture began to take him up. He had always had a weakness for Gentile, though his works, unlike those of his greater, more successful father, brother, or brother-in-law, evoked no dreams, no abandon. Gentile Bellini had painted a crystallization of the external reality of his age — Venice of the fifteenth century — and that was dream, that was "other," enough.

Marco knew that the picture had been painted as a type of medieval public relations. The leader (soon to be elected *Doge*) of the charitable brotherhood that had commissioned the painting, was portrayed as miraculously discovering and rescuing the Holy Cross from the canal where it had fallen on a previous procession. But the leader by no means dominated the picture. He was no larger, no more individually done, than the row of praying women, the group of impassive officials, the throng of monks on the bridge, each holding his candlestick at a different angle. It was a portrait of the Venetian people at their best, united in purpose, in industriousness, in confidence, in belief; the sense of community, of collaboration, implicit. "A commercial people who lived solely for gain." Certainly, but what they created with that gain. Over one thousand years of glory, the longest republic the world has seen, "The eldest child of liberty." Until Napoleon, they bowed to no one, conqueror, pope, or dictator. What they created. Not only the palaces and the *campi,* not only an excess of art and music, but an elaborate machine of government beyond the "irrationality of man." The nobility ruled and yet there were no titles; family was essential, yet boasting of one's forefathers brought a fine. Venice: well might they look confident.

"I've always wondered about that black man," the voice was close to his right ear. A young man, black coat, red plaid shirt, had sat on the bench beside him. "The figure on the right, peering down into the water. He doesn't fit. Why is he almost naked?" The man's hands were white and doughy. His face round, the features curiously flat. His moustache was so thin, it looked drawn on. His hair, however, was profuse: tight black curls reaching his shoulders.

"I suppose he's a servant," Marco finally managed.

"But what is he doing? Is he going to jump in or is he still looking for the cross, not realizing they've got it already? Dumb-like."

"I never thought about it."

"Well. I have. He must have been a slave. He looks like one. Did they have many slaves? Do you know?" He would pause slightly after each question, his dark flat eyes searching Marco's face as if he alone had the answer.

"I don't think they did. Not so late."

"I wish l knew more history . . . what *is* that man doing there?"

"Maybe it was a private little joke of the artist's. They do that."

"What about the men in the canal? They're like corpses floating there."

This was drawing out far too long. "Bellini probably wanted the connotation of resurrection. The painting is called *The Miracle of the Cross*."

"Rebirth in the canals of Venice. Descending and rising from the muck."

"It was a different era from ours, an era of faith and confidence."

The man's eyes were still, intent. "And now?"

Marco casually gazed around the room through the two doorways. "Now is the time of action."

The man turned back to the painting, "A time of terrible beauty."

Who thought up these lines? Marco stifled the urge to say that he could see the terribleness all right but not much of the beauty; transformation, that was what was lacking. He stuck to the script. "If the water is down, the demonstration begins at 16:00."

The young man turned to Marco again. "I never miss them — demonstrations, I mean." He laughed, his flat face crinkling up, like a picture on rumpled paper, his big body shaking flaccidly as he stood up. "Take care of yourself."

What could be the appropriate reply to that? You too, when the young man so obviously didn't.

The young man, now standing between Marco and *The Miracle of the Cross*, leaned over, bending from the waist so that his nose almost touched Marco's. "The beasts are awakening." He pulled back, straightened, but he left behind an unwanted gift, the disquieting odour of musty clothes and stale patchouli.

It clung — that smell — a brown gas tainting the air. It clung through several hours, all the way to Piazzale Roma where, finally, it was overwhelmed by the foulness of car and bus exhaust. The stink of the real world. Strange how often he found himself thinking that; each time he crossed the wooden bridge to Piazzale Roma he saw himself as crossing into the real world, crossing ill-equipped, "a fish out of water."

In fact, as he stood on the sidewalk, away from the curb, waiting for the 3:05 from Padova, a Fiat 500 which had been aggressively weaving its way through the congested traffic halted momentarily by a bus, paused, revved its little motor and humped its way onto the sidewalk. Marco froze, unable to quite believe in this car merrily speeding towards him. Incongruously, the driver was a large-headed, serious-faced, middle-aged man. The two other men waiting for the bus, in their scramble to get out of the way, had to attach themselves to the side of the depot. Just in time, Marco, feeling a bit too ridiculous, jumped sideways and flattened himself against the concrete and glass.

All of which was why he did not notice the Padova bus pull in. He looked up from brushing his clothes off and saw Paola and Francesco on the sidewalk about two bus lengths away. His heart, already agitated, took off, his pulse pounding in his forehead. How they stood out from the everydayness, the sheer normality of the other passengers. Paola had over-dressed Francesco, as she always did in winter on the few occasions when he was allowed out. A beige and brown down-filled ski suit encased his short, pudgy body, a thick beige scarf swaddled his throat, but it was the balaclava, covering all but his puffy mouth and eyes that contributed most to his extraordinary appearance. Francesco was fidgeting restlessly, hopping on one leg and then the other, flapping his stiff-suited arms in and out — like some mechanical space monster.

And Paola. She was dressed and stood discreetly enough, but the face she turned to Marco as he started toward her was not at all her usual, composed face; it was both tight and puffy, both distracted and obsessed, but above all, it was desperate.

Yet, as he moved closer, the desperation seemed to recede so that when he stood before her he suspected what he had seen had only been a trick of sight. In greeting, he let his hand brush her cheek where those deep lines had appeared. But Paola pulled back, instinctively it seemed, her eyes not meeting his but roving over the crowd. Francesco was grunting, pulling on Marco's coat. The father bent to the son.

Stella's Night

Stella wakes to shouts and laughter. She wakes to sweat in the crook of her right arm, behind her knees and under the hair on her neck.

She wakes to a heaviness of limbs and heat, to a wrinkled bed, this bed, where again she sleeps alone: husband gone, lovers gone, alone. The voices, the drunken gaiety, the snatches of rock'n'roll as doors are opened and closed, sound so close, as if the revellers are right outside her window. Yet, Stella knows from other nights, when she awoke to muffled knocking or to the click of a key in a lock and lay, heart pounding, convinced that this was it, someone was breaking in, rape and murder were on her doorstep, until she made herself peek out and saw no one was in front of her door or any of the other apartment doors on the second floor walkway; she knows how noise carries in the still night air.

She could keep her windows shut, the air conditioner on, lock out the stir of noise and air, but all day she moves in an envelope of chilled air, the car, the office, even her apartment in the evening, isolated by the severity of the valley summer. All day she longs for the moment when she can stand by the balcony door and feel on her skin the play of outside air, laden with the scent of bougainvillea and asphalt, with grit and hydrocarbons.

"A breath of the real" is the way she describes it to Alissa over the phone. She wants to add, "Everything is unreal with you away," but she doesn't let herself lay that too on her daughter's shoulders. Instead she says, "It's the job, you know?" And she doesn't lie; fluorescent lights, metallic coffee, the eternal roar of the air conditioner, the intermittent roar of the fighter bombers taking off and landing, and Stella at the computer: repackaging the numbers and words of others, reporting on the performance of machines to a machine.

She was happy when she started work at the base. Unlike the jobs she had while Bob finished his Ph.D, this was a proper job, one that Bob would respect, with security clearance and promotions and with a living wage. When he left he had spoken of how she must accept this opportunity to make a new life, and for months when she remembered the comment and his expression, she wished that she had spat at him instead of, as usual, swallowing. The seeds of his lush new life had been planted during the last two years of their life together. Before his little 1776, he accepted a job out of state, sold the family home and moved them all out of California, the community property state.

Only then did he make his Declaration of Independence. And once the documents were signed, money in hand, he ran back to California and to a waiting woman. The inevitable, waiting woman. If she had been able to produce no parallel man, the necessary basis for any new life she could imagine, at least, at the very least, she finished her degree, she got her job.

In the last few months her pleasure in the work, her sense of accomplishment at mastering what had previously been Bob's magical and mysterious world, the realm of computers, has faded. She comes home with aching back and eyes, with sore wrists and a dulled mind. And for what? Stella programs one machine with reports of other machines in order to service another, more complex machine — the military. And her service requires too many hours before a flickering screen, black lines pulsing on white, appearing, disappearing with one light motion of a finger, click click — here, click click — there, click — nowhere. Millions of bits of information processed into patterns of on and off magnetic impulses.

"It's nothing. When you think of it, nothing," she said to her daughter the night before Alissa was to leave for her summer visit with Bob.

"It's all in the way you look at things." Alissa's face and voice were edgy.

"Obviously," Stella said with a pronounced edge of her own. "That's what I'm trying to say." She regretted her tone as soon as she heard it. Her daughter was, after all, only thirteen, and, as intelligent as Alissa was, she still could not be expected always to understand.

Alissa's eyes were worried. "Put it away, Mum."

Stella touched Alissa's arm to reassure her. She made her voice light. "But then, when it comes down to it, we're not much either. Chemical processes, electrical impulses."

"You can call me there. If you get unfocused. You can. Jasmine and Dad are often out. Really."

I just bet they are, Stella thinks. They take my girl away to leave her alone, Stella thinks, alone.

Stella wipes her face, neck, and pushing down her nightgown, arms and breasts with a cold, wet cloth. The breasts aren't bad; the body, she reflects as she turns and poses before the mirror over the sink, is not what it was, but especially in a dimmer light than this one, it could still pass; it could still do the job. If a man ever saw it again.

If she could make herself try again. She had tried for over a year after the divorce. She had joined Parents Without Partners, Volunteer Action and a health club. She tried night courses, luaus, dance classes and bars; she met, dated and sometimes slept with various men, two of whom hung around long enough to be considered lovers and, in her mind, fiancés. The ride of the twirling flowers she called it to her girlfriends or Alissa: a little for a dress she wore then, red roses on black, low-cut, fullskirted, a look-at-me, out-on-the-town dress, unlike anything she had worn before; a little for all the bouquets and arrangements, roses, carnations, irises, daisies, daffodils, the odd orchid, a tropical plant in an enormous glass bowl and pots of African violets that the various men brought or sent.

But mostly she named the time after an actual fair ride, one that she had been coerced into riding by Alissa and her little friend. The three of them wandered into the small fairground by accident. Stella had brought the girls to the downtown park for an outdoor performance of *Midsummer's Night Dream,* but on their way first an overturned eighteen wheeler blocked the freeway and, then, in an attempt to flee the consequent traffic jam, she took an unfamiliar turnoff and got lost. When she finally found the park, the play was sold out; the opening trumpets were sounding. Stella was disappointed and angry with her own failure to plan ahead. Her mind was on what she should or could have done when she let the girls argue her into the line for the ride. And from there, the ride of the twirling flowers looked gentle enough; unlike several of the rides they passed, there were no sudden drops, no upside down flips. The young people were smiling; the odd shriek sounded happy. But when Stella's turn came, as she was twirled this way and then suddenly that, up and down, faster and faster, her sensations were anything but gentle. Disoriented, elated, frightened, out of breath, thrilled, raw and at the mercy of an unseen sadist who was pulling all the levers, that was how she felt out in the dating world. And both rides left her with wobbly legs, of mind or body, and a queasy stomach.

"Just you wait, you bastard." The voice is high and loud with anger. It pushes its way in through the high bathroom window and raises Stella's skin into bumps.

"Listen. Please listen." This voice is deeper: a man displaying his calmness.

"You said you would take me. You promised. And I waited. And waited." Yet another man and woman arguing. Usually there were more obscenities, more screeches.

Wait, the man's tone is growing rough with irritation. He saw her dancing, "his hand on your ass." Stella is amazed by what people say, amazed by what they will let others hear. When Bob had insisted on taking separate vacations, she'd said nothing. When he made his declaration, she let drop tears, not words. Even when she discovered that Alissa had known for over a year before her father left that he had a mistress, Stella's screams remained inside.

Only a couple of weeks ago, as she was putting on her night cream, she heard a group of girls singing a cappella. They were serenading a man, an elusive man, who was presumably in one of the nearby apartments but who did not answer or even appear at a window. Their tune was familiar, though unplaceable, the words had been written for the occasion. The song praised the man's muscles, his moustache and his understanding. Because of such attributes, he should forgive Brandy, one of the singers (identifiable by her "I'm-sorry, so sorry" chorus). "There's been too much clingin'/and not enough singin'. Brandy's going to reform/ or be stuck in the dorm."

Wasn't that the way, Stella thought, women doing all the coaxing and promising. He was probably fooling around, yet he made sure Brandy felt the guilt. Or maybe he was the type who simply disappeared, who one day was all kisses and plans for the future and the next was nowhere to be found. Then, the poor woman ended up examining her every word and action for the mistake she must have made. Larry, her first lover after Bob, had been like that. Stella had left message after perky message on his answering machine. And then, when he still didn't call and he still didn't call, she spent days composing a letter that discreetly begged him to tell her what had gone wrong, a letter which she had the sense never to mail.

The girls giggled before their song and for a while afterwards, waiting for the man to react, only gradually realizing that he was going to concede nothing. "The jerk," one girl said, cutting into the laughter.

"Should I knock?" Another voice asked.

"Again? . . . Smell the coffee, Brandy."

As they retreated, one of the others broke into the chorus of a current pop tune. And it is this tune which now echoes in Stella's mind as she sits motionless on a small stool in her bathroom, listening to the back and forth between the couple: the woman insisting that he had hurt her, how dare he grab her like that, the man that he had barely touched her, she blew everything out of proportion, she needed to calm down. Stella hears the words overlaid with a matter-of-fact rhythm. Anything you want/ you got it / Anything at all /you got it. Stella cannot move; she is fixed by the jagged sound of the voices outside, by the beseeching melody of the girls' serenade, by her own silence, years of silence.

Again, Stella remembers; again, her thoughts circle that evening when Bob still sat at the table, smoking his after dinner cigarette and telling her all was finished. She did not speak. The saliva pooled in her mouth. Right then, she wished, how she wished, she could cancel his words, that the right words or actions would wipe away his and the feelings they signaled, just as she wiped the remains of dinner, the chicken bones, the tomato sauce and the ashes, into the garbage. But she knew, as he said his first word, she knew that her wishes would change nothing. To plead or charm or sing was useless.

Bob labels her silence mature and realistic. Stella is pleased he doesn't suspect how much she wishes that they were still married. For though she makes lists of his flaws, though she reminds herself of his treachery after her years of compliance, she wants him or, at least, a streamlined, improved version of him. She likes the way they were before, early on. She likes how she felt: balanced, connected, satisfied, even though she can only identify these feelings now in retrospect and in contrast to her feelings now.

Especially in these hours, the late night, with Alissa away, Stella wakes more and more often. And she wants; she is paralyzed with wanting. She sits, listening to the sounds that intrude into her neon lit bathroom, to the predawn cries of birds, that instinctive shrillness. Her damp shoulders and arms are cool. On her left leg, she feels the lightest of prickles. Without opening her eyes, she scratches. The faint itch persists. Then she sees them — ants, a swarm pulsing at the crack in the corner behind the door, a broken black line across the linoleum, a trail of ants crawling doggedly up her leg. Her screech floats out the high window.

She jumps up, flicks at her leg: brush, brush them off. She swats at the floor with a kleenex box. The ants scatter, then regroup. Already a few are creeping up her foot. She opens and closes cupboards, under the sink, in the kitchen, but she cannot find the Raid. She settles on a lethal cleaning spray.

After wiping up the ant-specked foam with a paper towel, she returns to the kitchen for a drink but not even a full glass of orange juice clears her mouth and nose of the bitter tasting smell. She carefully washes and rinses the glass; any trace of sweetness will summon the ants. In her bedroom Stella checks each of the corners and behind her mirrored bureau, expecting a dark swarm. She has never seen any ants in this room, but when she can't sleep, she is often bothered by a faint tickling sensation that migrates from spot to spot on her body. And last night she did eat a chocolate chip cookie in bed. What if she missed a magnetic crumb? She snaps back the top sheet and shakes it. She bends over so she can inspect the bottom sheet while she straightens it. She flips and replumps her pillow. She pulls the top sheet smooth and tucks the corners in tight. Then she crawls back in.

The light around the edges of the window blind is grey. Already people are leaving for work; the opening and closing of front doors, the rapid click of shoes on asphalt punctuate the scolding of the birds. Soon, much too soon, she must wash and eat and dress, prepare herself for another day of work. But now, at this moment, sleep tugs at her body. On her eyelids black points dance on white; letters form and dissolve. She swoons into a drowse of desire.

MARY DI MICHELE

Les Plaisirs de la porte*

Women do not touch doors

They know nothing of its pleasures: they can only observe how it swings open miraculously as a man hurries forward and administers a sharp rap and then, sometimes, almost forgetting her, holds the door in his arms. She may rightly fear encountering its rough wood swinging back against her nose; she may, more rightly, put out her hand to ward it off.

If she catches sight of a brilliant world suddenly opening . . . he will enter before her, and if he waits and makes way for her, she knows how she must follow.

                    * A parody of a poem by Francis Ponge.

Necessary Sugar

For Emily

I watch you sleeping by the window
where the horse-chestnut lives,
its white candelabra blooms
aflame in the solemn mass
of the sun.

Giving birth I realized that men
build cathedrals in an attempt
to sculpt light,
you are the firefly
I collected between my legs.

A fiction that last summer's romance
had to write
for your father,
for myself,
not believing
love could be a lie
even if mistaken.

However the years tell this story to you
already June has ground up
the petals strewn across the walk
like a welcoming carpet for a queen
under the wheels of my shopping-cart.

My little bag of sugar, ten pounds,
I carry you in the corduroy snuggli,
my kangaroo pouch,
or the house a man might build
for his love to grow in.

The Wheat and the Chaff

A child growing out of your man's arms
like the miracle of flowers
around a prophet's staff
from a fifties' biblical epic MGM
starring Deborah Kerr and Robert Taylor.

You toss her into the air.
She is golden wheat in the thresher,
her laugh rises high and sweet.
Rich is the germ of our lives,
the rest is bran on the floor,
the rolling *r*'s of her laughter.

She's confident because it's you
who lets her go,
it's you who'll catch her again.

She will be the woman who can abandon
her body without fear
of hitting bottom or
the wooden floor with its glistening
sweat of wax
slapping her face.

Reminds me of a time before
I began sleeping under the bed

pushed out by the man who prefers
to keep his hands on glossy photographs
in magazines
or blond secretaries in high heels,
you know the type, hot little numbers
smoking cigarettes
or the long slim stems imported from France,
glasses of white wine.

Proof That I Don't Exist
(OR THE LOVER'S DISCOURSE)

He's not thinking about me as he
waters the dwarf palm by the window,
so green and alive in his life.
Yes, when he talks to plants they
blossom. I can see him cross
the room and trip
on the rug folded into a corner
so that the door won't stick.
One day he'll cut it to fit.
He's not thinking about me as the cat purrs.
Around his ankles for her supper,
the cat is golden and sleek,
the cat is an aristocrat and aloof
but low enough to beg for a meal,
I can't beg,
I would rather eat my tongue.
He's not thinking about me as he sniffs

his Napoleon brandy, I'm not French
nor a general, there's no trace of me
as he sips his five star cognac.
He doesn't need to know me to appreciate
that luxury. He's not thinking about me
as he changes his shirt, as he buttons
the little mother-of-pearl buttons of his best
shirt, the blue shirt with the canary stripes.
He's not thinking about me as he lights
another cigarette, when he draws
in the smoke, his body
relaxes without me, he burns
out his life in foul smelling ash.
He's not thinking about me when he looks
up at the night sky as he strolls
across Bloor street to his favourite bar,
in long strides with his arms swinging.
The stars have his shallow wishes,
but deep enough for me to drown in.
He's not thinking about me
therefore I don't exist.

Bloody Marys

You meet your husband at half-past ten
for drinks, leaving the daughter he donated
from his sperm bank with your mother,
he tells you about the woman who'll

sing in his bed tonight,
he tells you how her throat is adorned
with white camellias,
how she moves to his instrument
as a line of jazz,
totally improvised, always exciting,
and because you are never less
than a civilized woman, you ask her
name as you order another Bloody
Mary and shift uncomfortably
on furniture designed to be seen,
sitting out this dance around
the prickly pear, sex, the big
bang, then the whimper.

Simon Says

It was not love. What was expected from him, he could
only deny. Denial, she guessed she wanted it. She said No
to breakfast, eggs with their too sweet smell of frying in
butter, the yolk with its face of Anne Boleyn, executed,
white ruffle still around her neck, the home-cured bacon,
black gristle, all fat and salt like Henry. She said No so
many times, her cheeks darkened with hollows, echoes of
no. She felt as weightless as the subject of a hypnotist.

She didn't want supper. He was a grown man and she
was sixteen. He didn't call for her, she met him at the diner
for a coke. Then climbed into his pickup truck. He had

beer in the back and they drove to his place. While she undressed, he turned on the TV for the football game and opened a bottle. Nervous, she waited, keeping on her bra and panties. The underwire in the lace bra felt like an extra rib constricting her breathing. Her nipples were reserves of fire in the chill of the room. The wind turning back from the lake, the light turning blue as televison.

He was sprawled out on the couch, his work boots still on but the laces untied. He gestured her over, like a parking-lot attendant telling you where to go. She made her way to him like a child playing Simon Says. He was Simon. His fingers at her waist felt icy and damp from hugging his beer. Pushing her down into the couch and still watching the game. Pulling the crotch of her panties aside. Thrusting himself into

Theunderwatersounds

of the crowd. The voice of the broadcaster, an evangelist speaking in tongues. He sat back and finished his beer. The TV did all the talking for them. Then he drove the girl back to the farm, dropping her off at the dirt road to the house. "See ya," he said, putting the truck back in gear. As if his face were cloaked in the black, inscrutable hood of the executioner, turning away even as he spoke the words. "See ya."

As in the Beginning

A man has two hands and when one
gets caught on the belt and his fingers
are amputated, then patched,
he cannot work. His hands however
are insured so he gets some money
for the work they have done before.
If he loses a finger he gets a flat sum
of $250. For each digit &/or $100. For a joint
missing for the rest of his stay on earth,
like an empty stool at a beggar's banquet.
When the hands are my father's hands
it makes me cry although my pen keeps
writing, although my pen blots what's most
precious to me. Canabalizes this crisis.
To you my father is a stranger and perhaps
you think the insurance paid is enough.

Give me my father's hands when they are not
broken and swollen
give me my father's hands, young again,
and holding the hands of my mother,
give me my father's hands
brown and uncalloused, beautiful
hands that broke bread for us at table,
hands as smooth as marble
and naked as the morning,
give me his hands without a number

tattooed at the wrist, without the copper
sweat of clinging change,
give me my father's hands
as they were in the beginning,
whole,
open,
warm,
and without fear.

What the Light Makes of Us

1

Homegrown fruit tastes sweetest.
It matures on the tree and is not picked
green.
Fruit ripening in my grandmother's orchard
is not like the fruit I shop for
at Kensington Market.
I'll never buy back my exiled light.

The figs from California that sell three for a dollar
perched in pint boxes are not the purple organs
that glisten in trees like moist and naked women.
You might find that delicious shade
in the cavern of a lover's mouth
if passion were artist enough to paint
those religious frescoes of sex.

His fingers
when they touch
make me white
as the heart of palm.

2

It's snowing on the sun
sleeping in the skins
of oranges
piled in a cart.

The bloom in my cheeks
depends on these hand
outs from the south.

I stop to buy some and the summer
moves into a brown paper bag.

Nostalgia for the Future

A thousand mothers dressed in black
white handkerchiefs on their heads
silently circle the Plaza de Mayo.

They whisper prayers for invisible sons,
they want the earth that has swallowed
the kids to cough them back up,
they want the sea to return
what she has cured in salt.

The handkerchiefs ruffle like pigeon breasts
in the faint breathing of the square,
they never fly but carry messages
and names rewritten in invisible ink,
handkerchiefs fat from feeding on crumbs of hope
and women's hearts
held up like a sacramental wafer for all to see
before the unblinking eye of the government
goggled in brick and mortar.

The handkerchiefs seem to rise above dark heads
like clouds over Buenos Aires
and from their billowing folds emerge
faces of sons and lovers, almost reborn,
a facsimile of their boys, almost perfect,
almost come back to them,
an expectation that survives
like a beheaded cockroach
nostalgic for the future.

To Inherit the Earth

Everybody in Italy has a family!
From the film version of
The Garden of the Finzi-Contini

FORWARD:
TO SURVIVE IS NOT TO SUCCEED

1

Why do I remember it now, that line, from another time
and another continent? How are the atrocities committed
here in Chile mine? In transit, I view them. Victims of the
military regime tell me their stories because *they* believe
poetry tells the truth, because here even the military be-
lieves in books enough to burn them, because the relatives,
of the executed and of the disappeared, believe in charity
and justice that lives elsewhere. They tell me their stories
because they believe that the Good rule in Canada and
rescue will come like the cavalry at the last minute, the
cavalry in whose interest it is not to come. They think they
are only alone because the world does not read about
peasants buried in lime pits, countless bodies lost in loam,
in silt, the slit throat of the teacher, the bodies bound up in
the airfield, the bodies beached in the Mapocho, the mur-
der of the foreign news correspondent, the night raids, the
technology of the torturer, the housing crisis in Santiago
cemetery. The disappeared in the sea feed the *machas*, the
razorback clam indigenous to Chile, render their colour,

that peculiar and naked shade of pink. When these horrors are not *felt*, we eat them. Still the Chilean people do not see what stocks the shelves of our supermarkets. They think they are only alone because if these horrors *are* known to the world, then something is sinfully wrong. They count on the poet, part angel,

part animal, to be the one who
has not forgotten to feel. Whose words are secreted from the glands, words with the tincture of iodine, with the shock of insulin, with the bite of adrenaline, with the nuances of estrogen and testosterone. Words given us by DNA. So that what we are, and feel, and think, form grace/ful and inter/weaving spirals.

AFTERWORD:
TRADING IN ON THE AMERICAN DREAM

5

Listen, whatever I write here, what you read, is safe. It's between us. In North America writers don't disappear. They are not tortured. They are ignored. People are not arrested. They are illiterate.

Entertainment has become an industry, hybrid of boardroom and circus. How can we be touched by what the video screen dissolves into snow? It's a cold country.

Sitting on the floor, writing in my notebook, I can see under the table the network of spiderwebs holding up my printer. Displacement

is vision. How can we be touched? Two NASA planes from Punta Arenas, Chile, measure the damage to the ozone over Antarctica. There is a growing rent in the sky. The blue we will view as through O'Keeffe skulls. But not bovine, our own. Our skin and our children's will burn and fester. On the network the voice-over, with the gravity of an anchorman, urges the nation on. "To survive is not success!" it proclaims. Images of executives, Wall Street grey suits, Rolex watches, leather portfolios, men scrambling to work: "So America has been made GREAT!"

Over the planet the ozone is thinning, over the earth where to succeed is not to survive.

Bianca Zagolin

November Crossing

Forgotten by everyone, Aurora patiently marked off the days, without betraying her emotions. Life to her meant forever waiting, tirelessly: waiting during her sleepless nights for the break of dawn; waiting for her daughters to come home for lunch; waiting for the postman to bring her widow's pension at the end of each quarter; waiting for spring so she could plant flowers; waiting for something to finally happen, even though nothing ever happens in life; waiting for someone to come knocking on her door with an extraordinary piece of news that would gust through the house and blow away the dust from the years.

Waiting was her very own way of being: by the fireside, mesmerized by the flickering flames; on hot, sunny days, in the shade of the veranda where she sat in her wicker chair like a solitary grande dame, or at times of sadness, behind the curtains, looking at the street through patterns of lace. Waiting for the unexpected, for an increasingly impalpable event, without showing her inner turmoil. For the time being, it was enough for her to be strong and keep everything in order, not allowing the slightest change to alter her flawless universe, strangely akin to eternity itself. All she had to do was repeat the ritual gestures prescribed by an ancient myth about whose origin or meaning she knew nothing, but which gave believers, in exchange for total submission, a sense of the sacred. This myth, as all others, sought to make her bow to the mystery of life and death; by accepting to be part of the recurring cycle of things, Aurora could at least savour the joys of permanence. And so she put herself in the hands of the unseen powers that set the course of her existence, never failing to pay homage to them: once a week, she brought flowers to her husband's grave and made sure that, there too, perfect harmony reigned.

[...]

The cold weather came back, a hard, unforgiving winter that scattered snow everywhere and poured cascades of ice on all its victims without exception, not an invisible enemy reaching out only for Aurora with its icy fingers. An un-yielding time, but not without sweet moments or hope, a season in whose arms one curled up and which gave rise, along with incessant complaining, to a sense of wonder with each passing day. Aurora rejoiced over major snow storms, for these collective ordeals engulfed the whole city with her. What she feared the most was the sudden feel of winter when she least expected it, at the height of a sum-mer in full bloom, a sly, glacial presence that little by little numbed her consciousness like a dire premonition. But everybody's winter was just a few months to live through, nothing more.

No longer a threat, winter became a season of de-lights. Aurora loved the faint beauty of daybreak in the still of a freezing, grey morning, followed by a colourless sunrise whose feeble glow radiated through the darkened trees; or, at other times, the glistening snow on those days when footsteps crunched on the hardened ground as though it were about to split open. The constant glare, mingling with people's breath and plumes of smoke, made the whole city quiver and shiver like a giant mirage. After heavy snowfalls, Aurora liked to venture in the park and let her weight sink into the fresh layers of virgin snow. Instead of feeling oppressed as before, she breathed in the damp air, as a woolly branch suddenly caressed her with a sprinkling of fine dust. For months, the North wind blew over this harsh, yet beautiful country, her home. Once again, Aurora was captivated by the world around her, a world free of danger, forever unfolding its splendours.

But, in the light of her new-found happiness, the past seemed even more intolerable. Years of humiliation, swallowed with a smile, had stuck in her throat. She would wake up in the middle of the night, a prey to unknown forces; her thoughts would spin round and round in her head in a frenzy that lasted till dawn. Distant tremors were ruffling her still waters; their faraway rumble grew until it thundered through the recesses of her mind. Aurora had broken through the surface of her life, forever shattering the smoothness, and gained insight into another world where images were reversed. From the bottom of cloudy waters, she could see the hidden side of things. Her nights were haunted by weird apparitions, faces whose blurred countours stretched and undulated like the hair of a drowning man. Nothing was as clear, or as solid as before; reality seemed to dissolve, to run through her fingers.

Aurora now understood that rebellion had always lurked behind her submission, loathing often grimaced under a veneer of generosity; the joys of the past turned to rage. Her new passion for life had awakened rancour and hatred, love had unveiled resentment.

And so she floated in her own shadowy depths, where bitter memories tossed her like whirlpools of sea water, at last confronting what lay buried there, exploring the dark truths she could no longer ignore.

These unfamiliar emotions gave her no respite. They circled round and round in her mind to the obsessive beat of words left unspoken, words she should have shouted at the top of her lungs, for the sake of her own sanity. They were all gathering now, thousands and thousands of them, a long procession of discordant words, shooting forth like electric streamers in the dark. Her former allies wove themselves into nightmarish plots. So many words of hatred. Muted hatred, especially toward men, millions of faceless men who laid down the law and settled everything among themselves. Arrogant men who installed their constructions and cumbersome machinery wherever they went, who talked too loud and took up too much space with the awkward self-importance of precocious children, leaving a trail of incomplete sentences and unfinished tasks. A host of men everywhere, and yet always absent when they were needed. Her father, her husband, her brother. Men had offered her an arm to lean on, a roof to shelter her, children to keep her busy and a name to better define her. In exchange, she had renounced her strength and her voice; in order to be loved, she had accepted a life of isolation and fear in a world where no one expected her to do anything important. Thanks to Sebastian, Aurora could speak again and she was now learning the language of anger. Love had kindled in her the will to fight.

But Sebastian was a man. Would he get the upper hand like all the others? Would she hate him too one day, secretly despise him? The very thought of it made her blood run cold. Never. By wanting to provide for her, other men had taken everything away. They had convinced her that her security, her future and her happiness depended on them. With Sebastian, Aurora was starting anew. She felt as in her youth, when she didn't doubt for a moment that she could build her life with her own hands and her own will, and no one else's. Sebastian had restored her confidence and through him, she was reborn. It made her smile to think that she had truly become flesh and touched the good earth, there to reclaim her place, her rights, even the right to suffer and be alone, but to wait no more. She could never hate the man who had taught her that. And then, as in a vast loop, her passion closed in on itself, generating an ever-renewed circle of energy: the love which, at first, had so miraculously transformed her, was not the beginning but the end, the completion of Aurora's own joy at being alive, a joy that no longer needed love to exist and that became itself a gift to love. But she had to constantly watch over it, and be ready to strike at any obstacle that might oppose it and send her back to a self-effacing existence.

Her heart wavered thus between the quiet certainty of fulfilment and a woman's fury. Reality would then reverse itself again. Holding her breath, Aurora plunged into her now familiar depths where beloved faces were distorted and shapes distended, bloated beyond recognition, where truths no longer held and tender words turned to screams and lies. Gazing at this monstrous underside of life was the price she had to pay to finally resurface and bask in the light of day. And she did, gladly. People began to find her contrary, defiant; she had an aggressive tone, they said. More words invented by men, thought Aurora, to describe women who did not bow to their will.

After each successful stand, she had her strength to lay at Sebastian's feet, instead of offering nothing but frailty and helplessness to gods of clay. Aurora worshipped him. In an elaborate cult to his graceful beauty, she sprinkled perfume in his hair and draped his body in silk that enhanced his pale skin and the green spark in his eyes. When they parted, it was as though she stepped out of the light; Aurora disappeared once more into her dark, whispering shadows. But she no longer feared her own anger or resentment, or all the words she had failed to utter. Because in the end, there would always be the road, and at the end of the road, Sebastian, waiting for her. Her days were studded with memories of bliss.

[...]

By June, life was back to normal. Aurora vaguely remembered the events of the last few weeks; like a prisoner released after a long time in a dark cell, she met each day with a faltering step, blinded from the glare. At times, she felt she was no longer subject to the laws of gravity and her body, as though weightless, barely touched the ground. Objects around her were drying out, growing transparent, brittle as glass on the point of shattering. She had to proceed with caution in a fragile world made of screens, partitions and movable walls that could easily be knocked down with her fingertips. And death had weakened the power of words by driving them to the farthest reaches of abstraction; just as their arbitrary arrangement in crossword puzzles cannot create a meaningful whole, words didn't correspond to anything real anymore. They merely intersected without ever going to the heart of the matter, and Aurora used them one at a time, as it were, in an absurd and never-ending game.

Now that she had numbed her pain, she could at least do that, play the game. Aurora, queen in her own wonderland, would henceforth rule over a house of cards where tricks and illusions were the only reality. Yet on her cardboard throne, in her paper gown, she reigned with dignity, for her eyes had seen tranquillity and turmoil, reason and delusion, while her mind had found peace at last in the certainty of having nothing more to lose, on a path with no more twists and turns. Aurora had come to accept living in the present, a safe and comfortable place of which she knew every inch. She tore up her calendars, and thus freed from expectations, she was pleasantly surprised more than once by some happy occasion. Outside of obligatory milestones, time delivered its sweet moments. Yes, right to the end, Aurora would play the game, magnanimous Queen of

Hearts in a two-dimensional realm, forever one with her mirror image.

Translated by the author.

GIANNA PATRIARCA

Italian Women

These are the women
who were born to give birth

they breathe only
leftover air
and speak only
when deeper voices
have fallen asleep

i have seen them bleed
in the dark
hiding the stains inside them
like sins
apologizing

i have seen them wrap their souls
around their children
and serve their own hearts
in a meal they never
share.

My Birth

my father is a great martyr
he has forgiven me everything
even my female birth.

January was a bitch of a month
when i raised my head, for the
first time
from my mother's stained and
aching womb

a dozen relatives waited in the kitchen
to see the prize in the easter egg

how i disappointed them
my father's first child
was not male

i swear i can still hear the
only welcoming sounds
were from my mother
and she has always been blamed
for the mistake

for weeks
my father was drunk on red wine
mourning the loss of his own
immortality

Her Son
CELESTINA

i watched her fuss over him
as if he were a prince
an angel
a divine gift from God
her golden child
with the clear glass eyes
and natural curls
a perfect little man
with perfect little parts

and when he grew
i watched her caress his shirts
with her bent fingers
as she ironed out each crease
erasing any evidence of imperfection
i watched her fold each one
into a perfect square
buttoned to the neck
then she'd straighten the chest of drawers
and gently lay each piece of clothing
as if it were blessed
with such care and concentration
like the women in church who arrange the altar

i watched her prepare his lunch
the sandwiches always moist

the fruit always unbruised
and always something she had baked
for his male sweet tooth

i watched her slip twenty-dollar bills
into his trouser pockets
just in case
and when he allowed her
she would caress his strong cheek
bello mio, she would say
and then she'd place her fingers
on her lips as if she had let slip
some deep secret

she would look at him
and nothing else mattered
he could do no wrong

i watched her stare out
into a thousand midnights
waiting like a soft shadow
pinned to her lace curtains
waiting, for the lights of his car
to silence her heart
his footsteps up the walk
his key in the door
and then she would breathe
and disappear
i watched her love him
without fatigue

without expectations
then i would go
and iron my own clothes

Returning

we don't discuss the distance anymore
returning is now
the other dream
not American at all
not Canadian or Italian
it has lost its nationality.

In the sixties we came in swarms
like summer bees
smelling of something strange
wearing the last moist kiss
of our own sky.
We came with heavy trunks
empty pockets
and a dream.

I was one of them
tucked away below the sea line
on the bottom floor of a ship
that swelled and ached
for thirteen days
our bellies emptied into the Atlantic

until the ship finally vomited
on the shores of Halifax
there, where the arms and legs
of my doll fell apart into the sea
finding their way back over the waves.
My mother's young heart wrapped around me
my sister crying for bread and mortadella.
We held on
two more nights on a stiff, cold train
headed for Toronto
where the open arms of a half forgotten man
waited.

For Robert Pisapia
RESIDENT OF VILLA COLOMBO

you sit
flesh like stone
one leg less
a neighbour of death
your eyes draped by cataracts
they see me
but don't recognize
the face you smiled at
for years, across a small table
in the neighbourhood cafe

Roberto, how quickly
time gives a final embrace

last July we laughed
talked of your days of song
with Caruso
the climbing lights on the head of Vesuvius
the streets of Naples flirting in the night

it is a long way from Naples
to Villa Colombo

here, they have built you a fountain
they place your wheelchair by its
ceramic border
i know your ears are fighting
its fraudulent sound

Roberto, we will not speak again
until our eyes
are the stars over the
Bay of Naples

For the Children

for Laura
whose lips are mute
for her eyes
deep in their darkness
for her screams

at story time
the pictures
in her head
the knife, the blood
and her mother's arms
still forever

for Rosa
whose vagina
belonged to her father
for her shuffling feet
her resistance to laughter

for Michael
who is eloquent
with fists
and recoils
from my touch
from any touch

for all their stories
i piece together
for my own child whom i love beyond life

i am here

Sometimes in Teaching

five years of chalk dust in my hair
permanent dandruff
ink spots that will not wash out
on my only silk blouse

five years of Rumpelstiltskin
Rush Cape and Bobby Deerfield
at the lighthouse

five years of fractions
that will not be multiplied

five years of runny noses
bloody knees and hallway vomit.

they've called another staff meeting
we're all going to drown in our
own yawning for the ninety-seventh time

he is going to push a little
christian politics today
"we must learn to sacrifice"
there is little paper
we are out of crayons
only thirty desks per class

where do i put the extra bodies?

and i remember we must sacrifice

Michael knocks
"hiya, miss, you need any help?"
He places a sticky lifesaver
in the palm of my hand
"you're the best, miss"

and i know there will
be another five years

MARY MELFI

Sex Therapy

SCENE THREE

In *the room: Dr. Nicolas and Charlotte.*

DR. NICOLAS
I'm surprised no one's here yet.

CHARLOTTE
I had a dream about you last night. You made the cover of
Time magazine.

DR. NICOLAS
Many clients have dreams about their therapists.

CHARLOTTE
Are you married, Doctor Nicolas?

DR. NICOLAS
That's a personal question. I wonder why you ask?

CHARLOTTE
I simply asked, "Are you married?" I didn't ask, "Do you
belong to the Over-Endowed Society of America?"

DR. NICOLAS
Yes, I'm married.

CHARLOTTE

My last therapist suggested I was attracted to married men because I'm . . . well . . . self-destructive.

DR. NICOLAS

It's one interpretation. What do you think?

CHARLOTTE

Thinking is dangerous. If I think too much, I remember too much.

DR. NICOLAS

What don't you want to remember?

CHARLOTTE

Small things . . . like as soon as I started to wear a bra, my father stopped going out with me. No more movies. No more shopping sprees . . . Some of daddy's little girls grow up to be doctors or lawyers, I grew up to be invisible.

DR. NICOLAS

You became an actress. And a good one.

CHARLOTTE

I can't see myself.

DR. NICOLAS

There's a mirror on the wall. Take a good look.

CHARLOTTE

It's not my face. It belongs to someone I don't know. Someone who doesn't deserve to be happy.

DR. NICOLAS
Why not?

CHARLOTTE
She's not perfect.

DR. NICOLAS
No one's perfect.

CHARLOTTE
You are.

DR. NICOLAS
Most patients have a need to turn the therapist into an idealized figure. It's not necessary.

CHARLOTTE
What if I told you, Doctor, that I was in love with a married man again?

DR. NICOLAS
Would show a consistent pattern of response.

CHARLOTTE
Do I have the right . . . ?

DR. NICOLAS
It's not my job to judge whether it's right or wrong.

CHARLOTTE
You would say that. You have to appear non-judgmental, sensitive, compassionate. It must take a genius. Therapists are not trained actors.

DR. NICOLAS

I don't feign interest. And if it took a genius to be a good therapist, the profession would have a severe labour shortage on its hands.

CHARLOTTE

Do you like me, Doctor?

DR. NICOLAS

I like all my clients — especially when they're on time.

CHARLOTTE

You want us to need you.

DR. NICOLAS

I want you to trust me. Besides, I can't conduct a session unless there are at least three clients in the room . . . Where is everyone? The streets seem so strangely quiet tonight. It's uncanny. The silence has a certain resonance to it . . . Silence is a language in itself. Our eyes speak; our lips, our skin. And yet we often find ourselves shouting at the top of our lungs. It doesn't quite make sense.

CHARLOTTE

What if I said, Doctor Nicolas, I was in love with you?

DR. NICOLAS

Charlotte, clients think they fall in love with their therapists all the time, but it's not love. It's called positive transference.

CHARLOTTE
I've had over half a dozen male therapists. I didn't fall in
love with any of them.
*Charlotte is increasingly seductive; Dr. Nicolas is at-
tracted to her, but remains professional and in control.*

DR. NICOLAS
If there were a counter-transference — if I were attracted
to you — I would have to ask you to see another therapist.
Believe me, I wouldn't take advantage of you.

CHARLOTTE
How noble.

DR. NICOLAS
My licence could be revoked, Charlotte. Sex between con-
sulting adults . . .

CHARLOTTE
Consulting?

DR. NICOLAS
Consenting . . . Anyway it doesn't include doctors and
patients no matter what their age.

CHARLOTTE
Is it against the law for a therapist to fall in love with his
client?

DR. NICOLAS
Apparently, yes.

CHARLOTTE

Soon two adults won't be able to talk dirty in public. It will be construed as professional misconduct on somebody's part.

DR. NICOLAS

You should be grateful. A client's attraction to her doctor stems from his position. His power. I hope that with more therapy you will be able to transfer your affection to a more appropriate love object.

CHARLOTTE

Stop your psychobabble . . . Tell me do you like body jewelry?

DR. NICOLAS

Well . . . it is rather primitive . . .

CHARLOTTE

Who is more primitive: a woman who worships the sun or a woman who worships the almighty buck?
Unbuttons her blouse.
. . . Have you ever seen a nipple ring? Would you like to take a look?

DR. NICOLAS

I'm not a medical doctor. I don't look at my patients' breasts.

CHARLOTTE

Promise: I won't tell if you don't.

DR. NICOLAS
What if someone were to come through the door?

CHARLOTTE
Fear of having a lawsuit slapped on you doesn't act much like an aphrodisiac.

DR. NICOLAS
Doctors aren't invulnerable. They can be seduced. And ruined . . . Where's my briefcase? You can stay if you like.
Charlotte buttons blouse.

CHARLOTTE
I thought I was special.

DR. NICOLAS
I'm willing to be your therapist, Charlotte, but I can't be your lover. The roles are incompatible.

CHARLOTTE
Part of the job of an actress is the ability to make a fool of herself.

DR. NICOLAS
Believe me the role isn't reserved for actors.
Gets briefcase and coat.
When life throws a pie in our face, if we don't duck on time, we better laugh. And fast too.

CHARLOTTE
Can you drive me home?

DR. NICOLAS
I cannot, and will not.

CHARLOTTE

The reason I asked is because the subway shut down for the night . . . There was another riot — haven't you heard?

DR. NICOLAS

. . . My car broke down. I spent the whole day trying to fix it.

CHARLOTTE

Having financial problems, Dr. Nicolas?

DR. NICOLAS

It's none of your business!

CHARLOTTE

You're angry now.

DR. NICOLAS

I'm angry, but not at you . . . I don't understand what's happening in this *nightmare* city. There are riots after rock concerts, ball games, parades. And for what? A television set? Animals show more self-control. They don't go around rioting, looting . . . I better take you home. Old Nick must be having the time of his life . . . Are you coming?

Dr. Nicolas exits.

CHARLOTTE

Steal my heart. Loot my love. Abuse my trust . . . but don't kiss me off, Dr. Nicolas. Take me to the forbidden zone. I will be satisfied. Nothing will hurt . . . When a man and woman seek out each other's mouth they re-enter God's own mouth. Some call it heaven.

Office Politics

Everyone is doing well in my office,
nicely progressing towards becoming an authority figure
            Everyone, except me
I am singled out — might be demoted too — all because
            I wear the wrong clothes
        Actually the wrong clothes wear me out
            My suits are made of ivy
        Poison ivy

                        ∞

I'm unilingual   I can only speak Fear
to government clerks and unemployment cops

Is fear a language? Of course it is

Fear shows me up as a foreigner
My country of origin: the Leaning Tower of Babel

So my words don't carry much weight around here
                    Cash does though

But those who speak Fear, speak Poverty
and those who speak that, speak when they're spoken to

My nose breathes for me
My lips kiss for me
and the television talks for me

My closed-circuit circle of friends shout at me
but I don't shout back
I laugh and I am misunderstood
I cough and I am quarantined
I stutter: l-l-l-l-l-ove

Love is not a word in Fear
Love is a chemical — not like acid, mind you
Acid has power, and love for those
who speak Fear has none whatsoever

How pretty you are, someone lies
I nod and turn the other cheek

Everywhere I go smiles take up position
Fire at me   Shoot down my point of view

What luck: silence is a weapon too
I play with it all the time

Fear is my mother tongue
I shall always be in its debt   A true servant

But — wouldn't you know it? —
the sun races down from the sky
and paints my face a brave colour

ཉཱ

This city has so many walls,
                obstacle paths,
                                glass ceilings,
they make the former Berlin Wall
                (or the long-standing Great Wall of China)
look like a graffiti board

                They're everywhere around me
        Walls: reminders of how things are
                for those who aren't rich
for those who don't belong
to government-approved families
Appearance(s), titles, pet pedigrees count for a hell of a lot
                in the Walled Capital of the World
                                They have to
They're a new nation's building blocks

                Without money in my pocket,
        without a chapeau on my head,
                without a job,
        without a knife for comfort,
without identity
                I go from one wall to another
                                Beg for mercy
        (Or is it attention I'm after?)
                The walls in this city
        offer nothing
                                (for free)

                Hate literature

comes packaged in many different forms
Sometimes it's written onto an unemployment insurance check
                    but most of the times
        the writing is on the wall
                            In this city
the illiterate can get the message too
        Our walls speak (in tongues)

        The walls of my house use standard English
                "You are not welcome here," they tell me
                        "Rent due"
        No matter how hard I try
I can't shut any of the walls up
                Can you?

                        ໑໑

My mate wraps himself around the circumference of my needs,
        providing form and content to this ghostly thing
            which responds to my name:
            emotions,   body parts
                swimming towards the Unavailable:
                            the Divine

                    There is safety in prisons
            My mate imprisons my timidity;
        such delight in being his victim
        In his grasp: such prestige in being alive
    An overnight success: an island Queen,
a Manhattan cover girl — a beautiful hoax

My mate, my faith healer, my body tamer, squeezes me a little
    and a gorgeous perfume is emitted (household magic)
        Its sweetness poisons my sense of reality;
            sweetens up the everyday;
                suddenly I'm forgiven for my bad taste,
                    being average — an ancestral sin
        I want to be married
        to this foul god of indecision,
    be mated for life; I want him to be around
    my body: enclosing my greed, my lust in their
proper places — a live belt of sorts, a decoration
        to be worn to work — re-activating old-fashioned
sensibilities   (stability)

I want to use my belt — an alpinist
    hook onto safety
        and climb into the world of others
            Be satisfied:
            the universe was an excellent idea at one time
        Because I can wash myself in morning due,
            because violets lust for spring,
                because my mate mates in/out of season
                    because because because

There are medicinal properties in the familiar:
    familiar outlooks, conversations; roads
        Familiarity, Mate, I love the wave in your hair
        I can't part with your loveliness
                It propagates a special breed of wiry flowers
                    I decorate my belt with them

(good-luck charms)

Let's begin a wedding ceremony
between freedom and bondage,
between plant and animal substance,
Let's abide by the rules of the dictator: togetherness
I deliver myself to its openings
My heart takes a quantum leap   (Better buckle up)

CAROLE DAVID

Impala

7

THE IMMORTALS

Angelina had three sisters. All three had been separated by their father who didn't want them, and dispersed to the four corners of America when they were very young. My great aunt and her sister, my grandmother, came and joined a distant cousin in Montreal; the two others, Anna and Rosetta, were sent to stay with other relatives in Ontario and the United States.

I think I was able to reunite them because of a photo I found in her personal effects. Finally reunite the invisible part of themselves. They had been photographed before their departure, wearing buttoned boots, velvet dresses and big bows in their hair. A cheap cameo was pinned in the lace at their throats. An itinerant photographer, lugging his arsenal from village to village, had photographed them. The girls were between five and twelve years old.

Their father was a rich landowner who already had three legitimate children. He also had intimate relations with a young woman who worked on the farm with the rest of her family. One day he found his domain was getting too small and decided to send his illegitimate daughters to his relatives in America. Their mother stayed behind, resigned to her fate. She thought her daughters had left for a better world. She thought they'd live in palaces and make films in Hollywood with Rudolf Valentino, the great silent film actor who stirred the imagination of the Italians. What they found on the other side of the Atlantic was far from a fairy tale. Angelina was saved at the last minute by neighbors worried about not seeing her play outdoors. She had been staying with a cousin who had left her for dead with a raging fever.

My great grandmother tried only once to contact her daughters, just after the last war. She was not looking to Italy anymore for hope and happiness. The two sons she had kept with her were killed in the war. Angelina and grandmother had broken with their past some time previously. They learned of their mother's death through a cousin.

"Oh, if the walls of this apartment could talk," Angelina would often say to me, "they would have a lot of stories to tell."

But the walls of the apartment on the rue Drolet were mute; had they been able to say something, they'd have become as altars where each child, each mother would weep and tell of the things that cannot ever be forgotten. The sons, the daughters and their mothers would have made them into walls of lamentations. Their secrets did not cross the Atlantic. The two sisters had left behind what they had been, without ever saying much about it to Connie. They couldn't. They had sworn to keep silent and their memories were scattered through the new language they had to learn when they arrived in Montreal.

They left behind them parts of their lives in certain words; even forgot the smells, the feelings and the places which had been the very basis of their lives.

Connie had a garden in the backyard of the house on rue Drolet. We took it over after she left. We grew the fragrances and tastes that brought back her childhood to my aunt. After supper, Angelina would get down on her knees in the garden; she carefully pulled out the weeds which might smother the plants we used in the summer and all through the winter. I've already said my aunt was a stickler for cleanliness. She alone was able to keep up a garden the way a garden should be kept.

8

THE EVIL EYE

My investigation into the past, sparked by Connie's death and Angelina's departure, revealed much more than what the two of them had told me when I was a child and young teenager. I reconstructed, on the walls of the house, the family tree of Angelina, her brothers and sisters. How many of us in this country were seeking to know who we were? And all the ones abandoned in the U.S.A. and impossible to trace. I was safe and sound in the midst of my memories and trinkets.

My childhood dreams came back to me, but transformed. People came and went, opening and shutting doors. I could hear shouts and explosions. Voices would wail and lament and I'd wake up bathed in sweat, looking for the light switch. They'd start to die down, I would try to go back to sleep. I saw mutilated corpses, riddled with bullets, others floating in watery graves, or poured with cement into the foundations of a building under construction. Their faces appeared then vanished. The dead were beseeching me to follow them into the dark. I could hear their voices above the rustle of their bodies as they drifted past me. I knew that all that was left of them was their perpetual, endless coming and going, their restless torment come to haunt me the minute I closed my eyes in sleep.

ඉඥ

"You don't know who you are," Angelina repeats over and over again when I visit her. She touches at old photos with her wrinkled hands, murmuring prayers and incantations. She claims the *strega* predicted her future the minute she arrived in Montreal.

My grandmother and my aunt were convinced the *strega* could help them. She came from a village near theirs and had come to Montreal some five years earlier. Angelina still talks to me about her appearance: a scarf tied around her head, a shawl over her red satin pajama-like outfit. Her house was dark. She lived in a small bungalow in the north end of the city. The seance didn't last very long. The two women were scared, especially when they learned their children would always be pursued by the evil eye. The *strega* seemed to be familiar with our family history and the family histories of other people who had left the village. She gave my grandmother and Angelina two good-luck charms that would protect them, tied in a kerchief.

When I visit her, I always ask her to talk to me about my mother. She says it isn't easy. She never wanted to wear her good-luck charm.

9

THE LOST CHILD

We never talked about Connie's death. She couldn't bear to think about it even ten years later. Her life stopped the day Connie hanged herself. At first I thought she didn't feel anything about it, one way or another. I was mistaken. She obliterated it from her memory. She knows her life has changed somehow, but she doesn't think about it. She speaks about her past, her life with Franco and about a baby. "The baby I was forced to give up."

I learned of the baby's existence after Connie died. Angelina was thirty years old in April of 1945. It's strange to think the old woman sitting opposite me was once an unwed mother. Madly in love with a man who refused to recognize his son. She got married the following year to Franco, a friend of the family and who had courted her for years. As time passed, she gradually managed to make Franco believe she loved him.

Given her life before him, her husband was like a gift from heaven. He died before her. She found him dead in his chair one July morning. The Metropolitan had just opened a few days earlier.

After his death, she used to come and look after me when my mother was away. I gradually became her only reason for living. She had been there when Constance, her sister's daughter, was born, and now she was looking after me.

Life with Franco brought her nothing except security. He brought home little surprises every evening: a box of Moirs, her favorite chocolates, a brick of vanilla ice cream or some pastries. She would do her nails, get the supper ready while she waited for him to come home. The days seemed endless to her. There were special occasions, of course, like the weddings they attended on Saturdays, and the funerals where they met their friends and family, but that's about all life had to offer her. Nothing, not even the mountains of chocolate and ice cream, could make her forget the baby she had abandoned.

Franco and she didn't have any children. He always said jokingly that he had to take care of her. He knew the secret she so desperately tried to forget.

ర్యూ

I can't always catch what she's saying and I have trouble understanding her at times. There are places and dates missing that I need if I'm going to see her and her world clearly. Whenever I come to visit Aunt Angelina, she is seated opposite me in her black dress, her uniform for years now. Always the same one; sometimes, on Sundays and visitors' day, she spruces it up with a lace collar. She pulls her hair to the back of her head and holds it in place with clips. This is my enduring image of her, no matter how far back I go in my memory. When she was cooking, she'd wear a large blue apron over her dress. She doesn't need it anymore. Her meals are served up in her room because she doesn't want to come down and sit with the other boarders. My aunt lives with her ghosts. She has her meals with them, washes and dresses with them, and confides her secrets to them before falling asleep. Tuesdays are also the day for ghosts.

When they completely fill the room, I leave on tiptoe. Angelina continues her conversation with them after I'm gone.

She weeps for the son she lost, not realizing he has already come to see her. Her son had finally traced her whereabouts. Sylvain Hamel is the name he's carried ever since the day the nuns turned him over to the care of the Youville crèche. Sylvain Hamel's eyes are dark and he has an olive complexion. He thought for a long time he had been abandoned by a Mohawk or Abenaki princess. A princess driven from her palace and her kingdom. So he started his quest for his birthright. "It isn't much," he told me with a strange little smile.

After years of searching, he realized he was born in poverty. His past had nothing extraordinary to relate: no hidden treasure, no visible noble lineage, just a *mama* who had been abandoned by her parents like him.

Angelina introduced him to the nurses as her new lover. He took her back in time to what she used to be and that pleased her. She made demands on him that he took in stride, good-humoredly.

After a dozen visits, Sylvain Hamel didn't come back. She still speaks to him; he's somewhere in her room, among the statues of the Virgin and Saint Anthony, between two votive candles.

ANGELA BALDASSARRE

Chris Isaak

MILD AT HEART

Call him the Lone Ranger of Cool or the Zoot-Suited Sex God — some of us prefer Sex on a Stick - Chris Isaak can't escape the impact he's made in the music industry. With the chart-topping "Wicked Game," off his 1990 *Heart Shaped World* CD, Isaak thrust us into a dark and lonely world where love never lasts and where romantic memories of the past overshadow those of the present. This, coupled with a video of him frolicking in the sand with some goddess, rocketed the ex-boxer cum singer/songwriter/guitarist/actor from cult idol to international phenomenon within months.

Two years after the release of his last CD, 1993's San Francisco Days, Isaak came back with yet another brooding and melancholic Orbisonian collection of love tunes, *Forever Blue.*

"It came out of heartbreak," confesses the thirty-seven-year-old Isaak from his home in San Francisco. "They're all songs about one woman. We were madly in love. We exploded with love! I was in love with this woman and we had this wonderful, wild love affair. We were crazy about each other but she broke my heart. She actually tore it to pieces and threw them away. That's when I took off.

I went to Europe on tour, went to Japan, India, wherever, just to get away. I stayed away for three months trying to get my life together. I was devastated. When I came back that's when I decided to write the album."

Isaak has a tinge of melancholy in his voice as he talks about this massive heartbreak. One's definitely tempted to help him get over this phase. "Well, I'm happy now," he says. "But life is tough and I'm very emotional, very sensitive. I tend to dwell on things that aren't really worth worrying about it. I can't help it. When I give myself to someone, I give myself up completely."

The woman, whoever she is, should get her head examined. Aside from being exceptionally handsome and talented and versatile, Isaak is also one hell of a nice guy who bends over backwards to make those around comfortable and at ease. Remember him in that episode of *Friends* where he befriends Phoebe (the Lisa Kudrow character) and gets her a gig singing at public schools?

That's the real Isaak. This guy does not deserve to suffer.

"You know what my favourite tune on the album is?" he asks me. "It's 'Forever Blue.' It's a beautiful, almost haunting tune that helps you reflect on what's most important in life. You should try listening to it alone, in the dark. It's very, very lovely. It talks about unrequited love and how it doesn't matter how much you love someone, you can't force that person to love you back. It's a really thought-provoking song. But like in all my songs there's a reference to hope. The final lyrics — "No reason left for living / still there's a lot to do / new tears to cry / old songs to sing / and feel forever blue / and be forever blue" — deal with that."

For four years Isaak was in the limelight with concert tours, television appearances, a music video on constant rotation and small roles in big movies like *The Silence of the Lambs, Into the Night* and Bernardo Bertolucci's *Little Buddha*. For the two years before the release of *Forever Blue,* however, he disappeared.

"I was at my friend's place," he laughs when I ask where he's been hiding. "That's what I tell my mom when she asks me where I've been the last two years. You're always safe when you say you're at your friend's."

Seriously.

"I was traveling," he says. "I did a lot of traveling and touring with San Francisco Days. We went everywhere and I also decided I needed a break. So between making the film and touring and getting into trouble, I got pretty plastered. Then I came home and made this album in half an hour."

Now it's time to talk about his acting. How did he ever land a role in a Bernardo Bertolucci — one of today's most important filmmakers — film?

"Oooohhhhhh," he purrs. "The way you say *Bernardo* makes me think you're Italian!"

"Very," I answer.

"So am I!" he gasps. "My mom is Italian, she's a Genovese. Her name is Vignolo. That's where I get my good looks."

Genoa is on the Ligure coast, I tell him, and ask if he's ever visited this gorgeous northern Italian region.

"Yes, in fact when I was at Sanremo [music festival]. I took my mom with me and we had a blast," he says. "She hadn't been to Italy in years and we went around the town eating up a storm."

I wasn't aware that he ever sang at the Sanremo Music Festival.

"Yes. Even Madonna was there," he says. "In fact, the limo that picked us up had Madonna's list of all the things she wanted in her hotel room. There were pages and pages full, it was incredible! There was an entire gym, to begin with. It was ridiculous! She even had name brands of the type of equipment she needed. Then she asked for boxes and boxes of bottled water.

Stuff like that. Man, talk about . . .

So the question begs to be asked . . . what was on *his* list?

"Clean socks and underwear," he laughs. "When you're touring and playing you go through socks and underwear like there's no tomorrow. Who cares about cases of wine or bottled water, man. Give me clean socks and underwear and everybody is happy, especially my mother. Don't you just feel like a million bucks when you put on clean socks and underwear? Don't you just love the feel of the fabric?"

"Never mind that," I stop him before the conversation gets too racy (not that I'd mind). A competitive boxer before taking up music full-time, it seems unlikely that Isaak has much time for the punching bag these days.

"Just a little, but it's ruined my face," he says. "I have a fractured knuckle from a recent bout that I had and it's not worth the pain. I keep a heavy bag in my place, but when I tour I just run up and down a flight of steps to keep fit. I love to surf and there aren't many places in the world where I can do that when I'm touring, so it's important for me to keep fit. But boxing is really a dangerous game. They did a recent survey that showed that novice boxers suffer brain damage after the first three years of fighting. Three years! Doesn't matter how much gear you wear, it's the snapping back and forth of the head that throws your brain matter out of whack! Look at what happened to me."

Most boxers compete, others use their skills on the streets. Did Isaak ever get into huge fights as a kid?

"I don't get into street fights!" he laughs. "I'm a real chicken, a real sissy. I believe that if God had made me fast, I would never have gotten into a fight. It's because I realized I couldn't run, that I was an incredibly slow runner in fact, that . . . I thought I'd . . . better learn how to defend myself. But, no, I don't like to fight anyone. I'm terrified of violence, really."

Aside from the jokes, Isaak has strong spiritual convictions that have helped him cope with the sudden fame and continuing emotional turmoil that affects people who are in the career he's chosen. While making *Little Buddha,* the monk's story as a young boy, Isaak spent many weeks in Tibet with Buddhist monks, an experience, he confesses, that altered his life.

"It was a very, very difficult period in my life," he remembers. "I had just broken up with my girlfriend and one of my closest friends died while I was in Katmandu. I knew he was ill, he had AIDS, but it still affected me like nothing else before. So I paid more attention to Buddhism and the teachings of life. I realized we are only here on borrowed time. In fact, I always say that I'm renting everything because one day I'll be gone. I didn't convert or anything, but I began to look at life more seriously. I realized that one of the most important things in my existence is to make people I care about happy. People like my family and my friends. If I can achieve that, I'm happy."

"My work is what keeps me happy, being able to do what I love doing, which is writing music. Being able then to write about things that affect my life. All that and surfing and being able to spend time with my friends."

So what does the man who has everything still want in life?

"I'm not sure what I really want," he says after a pause. "I know I want a really good role in a movie with a really good director, which reminds me . . . I was in Los Angeles a few weeks ago and I visited this director at his house. We were having dinner with his wife and child, and I was looking at them and thinking, 'This is what the essence of life is about. This must be what happiness is really about.' I think that's what I really want."

Harvey Keitel

San Juan — Harvey Keitel has always been a journalist's worst nightmare.

With his monosyllabic answers during interviews and his disdain for the popular media in general, one has to wonder how different this New York native's persona is from his scumbag filmic portrayals.

Well, this writer was jettisoned backwards when the Keitel she encountered was both affable and cooperative, never mind cheery and playful. Maybe it was the warm Caribbean sun, maybe it was the joviality of the Puerto Rico International Film Festival, which he was attending, or maybe he was just in a good mood. Whatever the reason, the fifty-four-year-old actor was more than eager to talk about *Dreaming of Julia,* the film he was co-producing down here and starring in.

Pugnacious and intense who determinedly took on violent working-class roles in his early days, Keitel has probably had the most puzzling career in Hollywood. A sort of skid-row Frederic March (an actor he resembles facially), Keitel only recently attained the prominence he so richly deserved because of his unsettling qualities.

From the violent do-gooder (or badder) in *Fingers, Mean Streets, Taxi Driver,* and *Bad Lieutenant,* to the romantic brooder in *The Piano,* Keitel is now embarking on a sweeter, more compassionate path.

In *Dreaming of Julia,* an independent Puerto Rican production currently shooting, Keitel plays a feisty but passionate grandfather to a young Cuban boy on the eve of the revolution.

"I think it's an important story about the conflicts, the dangers, the chaos we encounter growing up," Keitel says about Julia. "And it's up to us to write stories about that conflict so we can help our children to grow up in a better way. That is primarily the reason I am here, in Puerto Rico.

Also, I hope to bridge a gap that is already being constructed between America and Cuba, a meeting of the hands that is long overdue. I think this project will speed up that process. Certainly it would speed up the hearts and minds of the peoples of Cuba and the United States to want to embrace each other."

As a member of the U.S. Marines during the tense-filled days of the Cuban Missile Crisis and the Bay of Pigs — "that was the last time I set foot in Puerto Rico" — Keitel is well aware of the events that have led up to the present-day embargo by the U.S. "I think it's time we ended it," he says. "It's gone on long enough."

Directed by Juan Gerard Gonzàlez, and based on his autobiographical script, *Dreaming of Julia* tells the story of an eleven-year-old Cuban boy in 1958 who suddenly finds himself without his beloved movie theatre after rebels blow up the town's power plant. The free time leads to all sorts of mischief with the boy's colourful family, his friends and the mysterious American woman, Julia, living on the outskirts of town. Once the power is restored following Castro's victory, things are never the same for the boy or the other villagers.

"The story is marvelous," says Keitel in his Brooklyn accent devoid of contractions. "It is a boy's coming of age and who of us hasn't gone through that, truthfully? The story has relevance to our society, relevance to establishing culture, that's what counts. The script . . . there's something magical about it, poetic about it."

Keitel knows first-hand about troubled childhoods. A survivor of a rough-and-tumble adolescence, he was thrown out of vocational school for truancy. He also stuttered. At sixteen he went to Lebanon with the Marine Corps and when he got back to the States he sold shoes. He studied acting with Lee Strasberg and Stella Adler from whom he got some parts off-off-Broadway.

At twenty-six he got into movies by answering the newspaper ad of a N.Y.U. student director, Martin Scorsese. Keitel was cast in Scorsese's thesis film, *Who's Knocking at My Door,* and then in his *Street Scenes, Mean Streets, Alice Doesn't Live Here Anymore,* and *Taxi Driver.* Though of Polish-Roumanian extraction, Keitel proved extremely convincing as a young Italian-American with conflicting feelings about his cultural heritage. Indeed, his role in *Mean Streets* is generally perceived as providing an alter ego for Scorsese.

In the late 1970s, Keitel's career suffered a sharp blow when he lost the lead in Francis Ford Coppola's *Apocalypse Now* to Martin Sheen after a falling out with the director. "The way I see things, the way I see life, I see it as a struggle," he says of that dark period in his career. "And there's a great deal of reward I have gained coming to that understanding — that existence is a struggle."

Over time, Keitel became typecast as an intense, back-alley thug (*Wise Guys, Bad Lieutenant*), a stereotype that proved impossible to transcend with his biblical role in Scorsese's *The Last Temptation of Christ.* (An apostle with a Brooklyn accent? Not everyone could see it.) But he finally managed to drop the thug persona (not to mention his pants), in Jane Campion's *The Piano.*

"Campion was a much tougher opponent than a lot of men," Keitel laughs. "Ability depends on the quality of the person, not the gender of the person."

He put in a strong performance in *Reservoir Dogs,* for a then unknown Quentin Tarantino, and his involvement in *Pulp Fiction* helped get that hit movie made. He and Tarantino reunited again, in 1995, for a vampire flick, *From Dusk Till Dawn.*

"Quentin is a brilliant writer," says Keitel. "I believe within his stories there lies a great moral quest. There is an ethic. I think Quentin has a distance to go before he calls out from his own material its very essence. He's just beginning. I support his beginning because he's a brilliant talent."

In fact, Keitel is developing a reputation for helping independent filmmakers, like Gonzàlez, get the financing and distribution needed to get a project completed.

"I confess, I'm not all that altruistic," he smiles. "It's the material that I find compelling. I can't resist a piece that would further my own education in real life. I feel it's an even exchange with young filmmakers. They're starting my journey into an area that is important to me and perhaps there's something in there unknown to me that I will discover as we proceed with the project."

One such project was Theo Angelopoulos' epic Balkan tale, *Ulysses' Gaze* which took over a year to shoot in the midst of civil war.

"When I formed my production company a year or so ago, I said to my people 'Let's try and go out into the world,'" remembers Keitel. "These obscure countries in Europe who we never hear from in terms of their talent... the talent must surely exist but America dominates the film market around the world. I feel the people of these countries are not getting the opportunities to have their stories told, their experiences of life told. For that reason, particularly, I'm here in San Juan making a film. Also, I must say, I have a ten-year-old daughter, and she has two godfathers, one is Robert De Niro and the other is Victor Jimenez, who's Puerto Rican. I feel I've come home in a way."

In fact, Keitel recently got caught up in an unfortunate scandal when he sued for custody of his daughter, Stella, by Lorraine Bracco. He accused Edward James Olmos, Bracco's current husband, of sexually abusing a friend of Bracco's teenage daughter from another relationship. Bracco and Olmos have denied the charge but Keitel won custody of his daughter.

Can't beat a happy ending.

FIORELLA DE LUCA CALCE

Toni

I

Must have been walking in the rain for an hour, maybe two, could not tell. Was too angry, too damn cold. Even though it was mid May, it turned cold nights. Did not mind the cold, really needed to cool down some.

Had another argument at home. After seventeen years of screaming and fighting you'd think a person would get used to it. Guess you never do.

Wondered whether to head home or not. Not that I wanted to. It was either back to hell or freeze.

The rain had turned to a light drizzle, leaving a thin haze over the circle of factories that used to be the old playground. A bunch of us would get together in front of the parking lots at seven p.m. sharp. We would play soccer-baseball for hours. The spunkier ones even found a hide-out on one of the roofs. Could not see it from where I stood. You had to know where it was to find it. The owner used to chase us out with a stick. We kept coming back. Finally bought himself an ugly bulldog. It put an end to our cops-and-robbers days. We were kids then.

A churning feeling started in my stomach. It gets that way when I do something I shouldn't. Across the street, all the buildings looked the same, except one. In the back was a long, rusty ladder leading to the roof. The only way up. I grabbed the bars, mouthed a quick prayer.

Hauled myself onto the roof, wiped my hands on my jeans and eased over the low stone wall. Sure enough the shack was still there. Hands and feet were frozen, my nose running. There was an empty hole where the doorknob should have been. It must have fallen off through the years.

The door would not budge. Tried ramming against it. The musty smell of decayed wood hit me full force. With blind fingers I felt along the wall for the light switch; remembered there had never been one.

Something scraped across the floor. My breath sucked in. Cold hands clamped around my neck. From the corner of my eye, something clicked and glinted, like a knife. Sure as hell was not going to find out. The hands became an arm. I sank my teeth into the skin.

He let go. I made for the door, did not look back. My chest burned as my legs scaled the wall. The dead taste of blood in my mouth made me gag. Heard the sound of running feet. Had no time to spare.

Stole a glance above. A figure loomed overhead. The ladder shifted. I missed the next step; came crashing head down against concrete.

My head spun. The blood in my mouth was my own. Rough hands searched my body. Someone swore. "It's a bloody girl!"

18

Gino drove like a madman through the lighted streets, hoping as I was that we were not too late.

"That was a red light you passed." My voice lacked control.

"You asked me to speed it up."

"Not if it means getting us killed!"

"I'm sorry." Gino lifted a hand to his forhead.

"Let's be careful," I said gently.

"I should have known that bastard was up to something."

"Maybe we should all have kept our eyes open." Nothing I said was going to ease the guilt I too could not help feeling. If only I had thought sooner of telling him we had seen Racasse. For some crazy reason a picture of Michelle leading him to the sidewalk came to mind and with it the haunting words: *If I said she will be there, she will be there. No one uses me without paying the price.*

"Look!" Gino's voice jarred me back to the present. We were back at the house. The lights were closed, the house silent. I stumbled out of the car, not waiting for Gino, towards the house. Somewhere beyond, the shrill thunder of the train echoed like a warning.

I ran. Gino called after me. Knew where they were — like I knew that Michelle had gone.

Two shadows rose and fell while another stood absolutely still a few yards away from the tracks. The earth pounded as the train rolled in the distance towards us.

Gino pulled me back into the bushes. His hand clamped around my mouth. The scene unfolded before us like some horror movie. Racasse had a gun aimed at Marco's head.

"Pa, no!" Renée voiced my own silent scream.

The man lowered his arm, turned to his daughter as if seeing her for the first time. Marco, seizing the chance, sprang to his feet and struck out. The gun sailed in the air. Marco reached out his arm. Racasse grabbed his legs. Marco toppled over him. They struggled, rolling across the ground, trying to grapple for the weapon. My heart clenched. Racasse's hand closed over the gun. I ran. Gino did not stop me this time. The figures became one. A single shot was fired. The sound jolted me backwards, and then silence.

My hate was no match for the man's solid mass. Racasse's arm snaked out towards my face. My back landed on the floor, blood ran from my nose. Racasse turned away from me towards the tracks. Renée's face was a mask of terror as her father approached her, her body frozen. The pounding of the train grew louder. It was not a freight train! It was not going to stop!

"Renée, run!"

As if struck, she came to life, saw the train and darted across the tracks to the other side. Racasse followed her. The cry died in my throat. Too late. The train sped on. I doubled over and retched.

Regaining my balance, I crossed over to Renée who was on her knees, rocking herself. I knelt beside her, placed a hand on her shoulder.

She looked up at me, her body racked by sobs. The haunted eyes tore my insides.

We held on to each other as we made our way back to Gino. He was squatted beside Marco's still form.

Was unable to voice the question. Had to stifle the scream that rose in my throat.

Gino's voice was grim. "We have to get him to a hospital."

We managed to half drag, half carry Marco to the van. Renée, who was in no condition to help, followed behind us.

"What about him?" Gino nodded towards the tracks.

Renée and I looked at each other. We got into the van.

Darlene Madott

Mazilli's Shoes

A Screenplay

43

INT. MAZILLI MASTER BEDROOM. DAY.
Giovanni rummages frantically at the base of the clothes
cupboard, searching for something. A suitcase lies open on
the bed, half-packed with clothing.

FRANCESCO
Flipping his car keys.
C'mon, Dad. The agent said two hours before departure.
Tony lies on his parents' bed, placing his order.

TONY
Bring me back about twenty *Ciao Roma* T-shirts, different
sizes . . . I'll screen *ciao* St. Clair on the back, sell them at
school . . .

FRANCESCO
I've put your Michelin guidebook in the outside pouch.

GIOVANNI
From inside cupboard.
I don't need it. I find my own way, with my heart.

TONY
Still musing.
The CN Tower on one side, Coliseum on the other —
awesome.

*The Leones enter the bedroom. Nonna Leone hands a
brown paper bag to Maria.*

NONNA LEONE
He never had a stomach for strangers' food.

GIOVANNI
Still from inside the cupboard.
What strangers? I'm going home.

NONNO LEONE
Home is where your wife sleeps.
To Maria.
What's he doing travelling without you?

MARIA
Apologetically.
A holiday.

NONNO LEONE
Good husbands don't take holidays without their wives.
Watching his son-in-law's rummaging.
You think I don't know?

TONY
Nah, scrap that order. Soccer T-shirts.

NONNO LEONE
He's like his old man, the sailor.

GIOVANNI
From inside the cupboard.
My father had nothing to do with me. I raised myself.

NONNO LEONE
Roots don't wander too far from the stump, no matter how hard they try.
Angle: Nonna Leone and Maria.
Whispering to her daughter.
You did right. Italy has always been Gina Lollobrigida for him. *Ma,* Gina Lollobrigida is only Gina Lollobrigida up there on the screen. *Non esiste.* Let him get close. He'll see she has wrinkles and sagging boobs.
Close up of Maria's Face. Uncertainty.

DIANA
Who's Gina Lollobrigida?

GIOVANNI
Ecco. Now I can go.
He emerges from his search with an old pair of black leather shoes. Fondly, he rubs the dust off the shoes, and lays them in the suitcase on top of his clothes, soles up.
Tony picks up a shoe and examines it.

TONY
You're taking these?

GIOVANNI
A gift from my mother. She bought these shoes with money she didn't have. I promised her someday I'd wear them back.

TONY
They're going to hurt.

GIOVANNI
A man should keep his promises, even if they hurt . . .
especially if they hurt.

*Decisively, Giovanni snaps shut the suitcase. He turns
and seeks out Maria. He goes to her. Beat, as they look at each
other. Giovanni locks her in his arms. Then he picks up the
suitcase and heads out the door with Francesco.*

44

EXT. ITALY, SPRING. MORNING.
*Aerial Travelling Shot: A Train is threading its way
through a spectacular and sunlit countryside toward the
coastal town of Vasto.*

45

EST. TRAIN STATION. VASTO, ITALY. MORNING.
*The train pulls into the station. A number of people
disembark, met by family and friends. Then Giovanni emerges
into the frame of the train doorway, looking dazed and disori-
ented. He squints at the dazzling sunlight with unaccustomed
eyes.*

CABBY'S P.O.V.
*Giovanni is an oddity. He lugs a heavy suitcase and
carry-on-bag, is dressed in Canadian tourist's clothing, but
with the old Italian leather shoes. The first few steps Giovanni
takes on the platform indicate he's in some kind of pain. He is*

hobbled by the shoes. He bends down to pick something out of a shoe. The bus into which the recent arrivals have loaded themselves, takes off in a cloud of dust and stones toward town. Giovanni misses it. When it passes, he emerges from the dust, straightening himself. He is thoroughly pissed off at the moment's delay over a shoe that cost him the ride into town.

Driving his cab like an extension of himself, the Cabby (Antonio Tassista) pulls over to where Mazilli stands. He hops out, throws open the cab's trunk and grabs Giovanni's suitcases. Instinctively, Giovanni hangs on, and blurts out in English.

GIOVANNI
What are you doing?
They engage in a tug-of-war over the luggage.

CABBY
I help. You got somewhere to go? I take you.

GIOVANNI
I've arrived. I know where I am. I don't need your help.
The Cabby looks crestfallen, as if this is a personal affront.

CABBY
You going to walk from here?
Giovanni considers the hill, then his feet. Profiting from his indecision, the Cabby succeeds in extracting the suitcases from Giovanni and tosses them into his trunk.

CABBY

Antonio Tassista at your service. You need something? A
place to stay? I know everything there is to know.

GIOVANNI

Shoes.

CABBY

Shoes? This, too, we can arrange.
Cavalierly, he opens the cab door for Giovanni.

46

INT. CAB. MORNING

GIOVANNI

So where did you learn English?

CABBY

In prison. By correspondence.

GIOVANNI
Nervously.
Yeah? What did you do?

CABBY

Me, nothing. *They* defamed me. They said I had . . . how
do you say? —*fatto il palo.*

GIOVANNI

Oh, you were the get-away-man.

CABBY

These two guys wanted me to drive them to Chieti and wait. A little later, they come out with a bag. They tell me to drive fast. After, if they were so good to give me 500,000 lire, why shouldn't I take it for that kind of service? There's no law against gratuities.

As the cab heads up the coastal hill into town, Mazilli gazes at the surrounding sea and then the town. He loves it. He doesn't know which window to look out first, as frisky as a child going on his first picnic in the country.

They mount the hill; the view opens.

GIOVANNI

Halt!

The Cabby slams on his breaks. Excitedly, Giovanni scrambles out of the cab and out onto the meadow overlooking the valley.

47

EXT. HILL OVERLOOKING THE VALLEY. MORN-ING

Giovanni takes a deep breath and spins around, his arms open.

GIOVANNI

What a panorama. Finally, I can breathe again.

CABBY

Watching him from the cab, calls out.

So how long have you been holding your breath? What part of the planet do you come from?

48

INT. CAB. MORNING.

GIOVANNI
Directing his driving.
No, not this way. Through the centre of town.
They enter the city limits.

GIOVANNI
Peep your horn, like it's a wedding.
Giovanni hangs out the window, waving and smiling like a passing dignitary. Local townspeople look up and watch the passing cab with curiosity. An old man, grinning tooth-lessly, waves back.

49

EXT. VASTO. TOWN CENTRE. DAY.
The taxi takes Giovanni to Vasto's downtown. It consists of a square, with a fountain, the town clock — the village monument. Fronting onto the square are merchant's shops.
Giovanni gets out of the cab and hobbles over toward the fountain.

CABBY
The meter is running.

GIOVANNI
Let it run.
Giovanni takes off his shoes and socks and climbs into the fountain, sighing with satisfaction as his feet hit the cooling waters. He reaches down with his hands and baptises himself,

splashing water over his face and head. Again, local reaction.
Giovanni laughs and waves. Townspeople wave back indul-
gently, as if to say: "Crazy tourist, let him have his fun."

50

EXT. SHOE SHOP. DAY.
The Cabby pulls up behind a bus, across the square from
the shoe shop.

MAZILLI'S P.O.V.
Close on store front: DiPasquale Calzature.

GIOVANNI
I can't believe my eyes. It's still here.
A jubilant Giovanni steps out into the square, and is
nearly run over in his wild excitement to make contact with
the past.

GIOVANNI
Wait for me.
The Cabby scrambles out of the cab after him.

CABBY
I don't wait anymore.

TIZIANA BECCARELLI-SAAD

Fable

"Nowadays," the man said, "it seems that it is the children who come to their parents' rescue."

The mother looked down and didn't say anything. She hasn't had much to talk about lately. As she sighs, there is a bitter taste in her mouth. Her eyes are filled with a permanent sadness. A few moments later, feigning a migraine, she exits the dining room.

"Yet again," she tells herself trembling.

Ever since they moved in, she has been unable to deal with her son and her daughter-in-law, not to mention her own life. And things are getting worse. She doesn't have to search very deeply in her internal album of treasured family memories to find the strength to forgive her son's latest spiteful deeds. But as for her daughter-in-law: not a chance! She does not have a single happy recollection to help cushion the latter one's latest petty offense. The mother now just closes herself up in her dull and miserable room. Having nothing else to do, she quietly contemplates her death which she hopes will come soon, if only to put an end to this inner corrosion she senses, pretending that living one more day is a matter of choice.

No, it's impossible, she says to herself, to be exiled in one's room, doors and windows sealed shut, pretending that the world outside does not exist. You can't help but take it with you.

The pain she feels in her gut only gets worse the harder she tries not to think about it. For some time now, as she observes Victor around the house acting as though she did not exist, she is dismayed by the thought that this child of her womb places greater value on money than he does on people. She hates having to be judgmental towards her son for what he has become.

This only shows how insidious love can be; it makes you betray your principles, she thinks as she stares at the wallpaper.

How then to describe the nature of the love she feels for her son? Why does she love him? He shares no traits with his father, neither moral nor physical. Victor often demands quite openly to be flattered and admired. He compels his mother to play his game with his pitiful ruses. She has tried to resist, but she gets tired and inevitably gives in. Their relationship has since lost all sincerity. She tries to detach herself from him by never laying eyes on the pictures of the plump and tender infant that Victor once was. She feels the urgent need to remain silent whenever she is in the presence of her son and her daughter-in-law. Both are thankful for her muteness. She knows that after she leaves the room they take pleasure in ascribing her silence to senility. She would have given so much not to see her son transformed into the two-legged monster he has become. There is a knock on the door.

"Mother, Mother! What are you doing? Come, Victor has a charming surprise for you in the living room. We're waiting for you!"

Against her will she detaches herself from her solitude. The people in the living room are friends of Victor's. He goes to such great lengths to show everyone he is taking care of his "dear old mother" that she tells herself at least they both share a very impractical vice: he, too, overdoes it.

She repowders her nose, puffs her hair and walks in a dignified manner towards the living room. Her entrance is not noticed in the least. Feeling pleased about this fortunate circumstance, she sits on the chair in the back of the room: the one withdrawn from the rest and also the one she used to reserve for her impoverished cousin during family gatherings when she used to reign over her household.

"The fact is that his faithfulness obliges me to be faithful as well," says her daughter-in-law and suddenly bursts out laughing.

The mother feels herself closed like an oyster. Her daughter-in-law's excesses are always dumped on her. After the laughter subsides, a thick silence invades the room. She knows that silence can burn. Her son notices her; he scrutinizes her. His eyes cross hers; soft and sad eyes, eyes so sad that they seem to be reproaching him for having prevented sleep from closing them for a few hours.

"So, Mother! You seem to forget us more and more."

Yet another well-aimed arrow which knows which part of the body it should wound. The mother understands her son's painful need to annihilate the evidence of his powerlessness: the powerlessness of having failed to live up to her expectations, of having failed to amend his weaknesses. And so, he wounds.

"He who has no trouble loving has no trouble punishing," she sings to herself softly.

"Your mother is a very joyful woman, Victor." It is the engineer speaking, Victor's friend, the one with such nice hair. He thinks she is joyful because she is singing. Yes, of course, these are all people who take satisfaction in noticing such obvious things.

"Mother, this is for you." He hands his mother a key. She seems surprised. He insists. "Well, Mother? Don't tell me you have forgotten again. Come now . . . Move in a little closer. Mother, we have spoken about this quite at length . . ."

She puts his fingers on her lips. She stiffens as she stands up. It doesn't matter anymore. Suddenly, it becomes imperative that she leave before she rots completely.

"Well, Son. When do I leave?"

Satisfied, he takes his mother's hand and spins her like a child.

"Behold my mother, behold the being who made me. Courageous, determined . . ."

"And old!" the daughter-in-law cuts in, irritated by her husband's excessiveness.

"Very old. If you will pardon me, I shall retire. Ah, Victor. Remind me a few hours or so before it is time to go. I have to go through some souvenirs I'd like to bring with me."

She turns to the others: "Good night. Enjoy your evening."

Before going to her room, she stops by the kitchen. She thinks of Ginette, the cleaning lady, and her hiding places. She knows all of them. The laughter in the living room dies down as she closes the door of her room. She lies on her bed. I belong to a family that has abandoned me, she tells herself without much sadness.

She gets up and goes to the bathroom. She washes meticulously and puts on her night clothes. Lying down again, she leans over and takes a "damned glassful," as her dead husband would say, of port, which she pilfered from Ginette. She drinks neither for pleasure, nor out of vice, but simply to forget. Her mind is putting up some resistance. Another gulp! One less bottle for Ginette. During these periods, life seems so difficult. She has yet to learn how to come to terms with her past; that notion of things "having been" so beautiful, so full, so complete. And if she glances ahead towards her seemingly shapeless future, it nevertheless seems to her that she is being whisked further and further away from her true nature, further from herself, only to be plunged in that confusion we sense when we do not know ourselves.

She sees herself condemned to move forward across the unknown and inexorably towards her death.

"The fool loves to teach while the cunning man prefers to be taught."

Victor, it is quite plain to see, is about to explode. His wife cannot stop glancing at him and smiling. Clearly, she admires the engineer's technique. He brings Victor to the brink of anger and catches him just before it turns into hatred — enough to compel him to remain cordial.

"Your father's pretension, his legendary selfishness . . ."

The voice gets lost in the sudden thunder of noise. The hosts cover their ears.

"Victor, can't we do something?"

"No, my dear. Nothing at all."

Victor is glad the explosion of sound coming from the neighbour's apartment interrupted the engineer. He looks at his wife deliberately while the guests stare at the carpet flowers. He is fascinated by her beauty, a perfect beauty, almost inhuman. Why does he so often feel manipulated by her. What, if anything, is she thinking? A beauty beyond compare upon which her entire being rests. How dare he try to trouble her? Can he really unmask her? He only knows that after all this time spent sleeping beside her, the sensation of novelty has never been replaced by repetition. Finding her every night in his bed, he apprehends an infinity of fresh starts. Victor breaths easier. He sighs. Thinking these thoughts makes him feel sheltered and more secure. Already his anger at the engineer and at his wife is dissipating. The mood in the room is once again serene. The people in it quietly and politely engage in the ritualistic gestures such circumstances require. Their tone is ordinary. These are not the kinds of people to be concerned by petty things such as jealousy or envy. The pleasant mood now permeating the room brings the evening to a more gentle conclusion than might have been expected only moments before. But if Victor had been more alert, he would have noticed the engineer whisper in his wife's ear.

"I've got my eye on you. I'll be your bodyguard."

And if she hadn't been so sure of herself, she would have noticed the smile painted on his lips, an unpleasant smile.

A few hours into her sleep, the mother awakens. It is still dark. Her head aches. I must once again rip out of my mind these roots that are still so alive, she tells herself.

She wishes she could stop her internal film. Even drunk, the images keep coming back, haunting and marvelously fresh. How could she not have foreseen what Victor would have become? Where did she go wrong? Where did the evil come from? By whom did it come? By whom. She chases away the name as it comes into her mind. If Victor ever found out, he would be capable of beating her. They had spoken about it, a long time ago, before his marriage. Their quarrel is clearly etched in her memory.

"Victor, you are an innocent fool. How can you stand there and be awestruck by her outward appearance and assume that she is the same on the inside? Any idiot is wise enough not to fall into her trap. That woman is far from being transparent, and fundamentally you know it, too."

"Mother, you have a totally erroneous way of understanding the world. You imagine certain things only because your life was so easy and comfortable. That is all you have ever known."

"And what about your life. How did I make your life? Difficult, perhaps!"

"No, of course not. But I have a greater experience than you with other ways of seeing, other realities."

"And you think your judgment is better only because of that! Hasn't it ever occurred to you that all the things you think you see, you only see because you have misunderstood the situation? You misinterpreted what is going on?"

"What do you expect from me? That I leave her?"

"I would simply like that you take the time to learn certain things before thinking about getting married. Learn to rely on yourself, for example. You are trying to fill your emptiness by putting faces to your encounters. But the emptiness remains, hidden for a while maybe, but soon it resurfaces! Like a weather vane, you go in the direction of whichever wind is blowing. Victor, be consistent, give yourself instead of taking all the time. If you should leave her, do so for yourself, in your own best interest, not for anything else."

"You know what, Mother. I think you're jealous."

He left the room. The matter was closed. A few months later he came to live in the house with his new bride. Her hell began on that day.

Sleep refuses to take hold. The temptation is great to take the tiny white and pink tablets prescribed by her doctor.

"Not more than two, Madam, simply to help you relax."

She is lying there, waiting for the break of day. Waiting for what, after all? She remembers that Victor will get rid of her soon. He planned everything carefully. A blinding rage takes hold of her. She is angry at being so old. Her body is old, but not her mind. "You are old, you are old," her body tells her repeatedly. But her mind refuses to acknowledge the evidence.

She stands by her window and looks up to the sky. Her thoughts follow the course of the clouds, vague and imprecise. Finally dawn. She is now perfectly calm.

It is now almost ten o'clock. Victor is sure to find his mother awake. He would have preferred to wait another month or two, but he could no longer hold out against his wife. Finally, he gave in. Bitter thoughts of the night before plant themselves in his gut and cause his legs to feel weak. He cannot bear to think about his wife's indifference and her barely disguised contempt. And that engineer who calls himself his friend . . .

He knocks on the door and goes in. His mother is lying on the bed fully dressed. She seems completely at peace, almost as though she is wearing a masque. He draws nearer and shakes her gently. On the night table there is an envelope. He opens it and reads.

On what malevolent pleasure did such a young and beautiful woman feed? And why did she feel so threatened by the tenderness which united the old lady to her son? Day after day the old lady stumbled on some new trap set by her daughter-in-law, but she did not dare complain to her son for he only looked at her menacingly and treated her brutally. So the poor old lady circumscribed more and more the territorial range of her daily activities, simply to avoid falling into another trap set by either one of her executioners.

She ended up occupying just one room of a large dwelling: her bedroom. This inactivity caused her head and her heart to atrophy, so much so that she prayed for a speedy death lest her decline be even greater.

In the meantime, the house became ever more filled with venom. The daughter-in-law's contempt for the old lady was ferocious and complete. Even the old lady's invisibility angered her. She set deadly traps that the old lady eventually could not escape. In all this, the son had had but one weakness. It was only one, but it was an enormous one; his concupiscence. His nights had been an endless merry-go-round of lustful encounters with the young pearls in the neighbourhood; until the day when a woman refused to give herself to him. A woman of cunning, no doubt, she showed him the way to the altar. He followed her without so much as a whimper. He had found woman and master. But here was the catch, for even after the wedding, she did not give herself to him. She tortured him, and did with him what she pleased. Night after night she repudiated him stubbornly and indifferently. It drove him to the point that he could no longer think rationally. He began to hate his mother. He began to hate his own life and himself for being so poorly armed against the fickleness of such a young and beautiful woman. Just when the woman in question sensed that he was beginning to crack, she turned to him and said: "Go! Take your old mother into the forest and kill her! Put her head in a pouch and bring it back to me as proof of having accomplished the deed."

The man, tortured as he was by his desire for the woman's body, knocked on the door of his mother's room. "Mother, come!" he said. "It is a beautiful morning. Let us go for a walk in the woods."

The old lady, only too happy to listen to her heart, let herself be taken along. In the pleasant tranquillity of nature, away from the eyes of men and close to the eyes of God, the son cut off her head.

The road back was difficult. Remorse, absent until then, began to creep into his heart until it overwhelmed him. Nearing the bend, the son tripped on a tiny stone protruding from the ground. He accidentally dropped the pouch causing the bloody head to roll out. Terrified, he tripped again and fell to the ground near where the head had stopped rolling. As the son wiped his hands on his sides, the old head covered with blood turned to him and said: "There, there, my son. You didn't hurt yourself, I hope!"

Translated from the French by Domenic Cusmano.

CONCETTA PRINCIPE

Stained Glass

Winter 1990, she met Christophe. Nomad Gallery. She was there with a gang of others to support one of her roommates, Michael, who's iron totem was in the show.

The studio swarmed with bodies, artists, critics, bad artists, closet critics; the studio smelled of turpentine, smoke, black leather, beer, and hash; and the only deals going down were for drugs, and the other cash going round was for beer.

X was standing by the windows. Behind her Michael's primitive totems glowed an uncanny blue in the light of the neon-abstract suspended on the wall: shadows quivered there, alive.

A shadow moved. Turning she saw the totem smile, spilled her beer. "God damn it," she said.

"God doesn't give a damn," the totem said. A man. Christophe. The first thing Christophe said to her. The first thing she noticed was the color of his skin, then the shadows out of which his eyes gleamed.

Later, Natalie asked, "So . . . who's he? Your latest conquest, or your deepest darkest secret?"

"What?"

"Are you fucking him?"

"Natalie, don't be crazy, we just met." X looks at Natalie not seeing.

How Natalie touches herself, absentmindedly, three fingers along the lycra dress cut low enough to show some breast, pausing at the collar bone: a Pre-Raphaelite model scanning the crowd for the painter who will become her lover with whom she can engage in a politics of sexual power.

X wasn't seeing anything but the image in her mind's eye. The portraits she had painted last summer. All of them, the spitting image of Christophe.

ဢ

If she was destined to meet Christophe through Michael, because Michael knew everyone it seemed, was she destined to know Christophe the way she did? Did she invent him? Or was he all there was: the diffidence?

This was 1990. The plague had hit relationships, and couples were coming apart left right and center. Leaving everyone single; everyone mad for sex; everyone wary of love.

What goes around comes around. What had she given the man who did love her? Not the words, "I don't love you," because they might have been a lie. Not the explanation, "This is an affair that should have ended when it began," because maybe it wasn't true. Just a vague excuse, "I'm not ready for marriage yet."

Who was? Who is, ever? And if they are, is it love?

Love, like marriage, dies. But better love should die than marriage: separation, custody, the divorce she knew at ten, which Christophe also knew.

Was she looking for a man she could know? Christophe, son of an Irish woman and French Algerian man; because she knew what it was like to be divided inside, to grow up divided between parents, families, languages; her Italian father, Irish mother.

Was this destiny? That she could read him. What she read in his eyes, a promise: "If you would love me." How she felt with him, what she had never felt before: the desire to have a child.

The diffidence. Who he was: a man, fifteen years her senior, on welfare, who had nothing but his poems and his heroin. Who she was: a woman in her twenties who had nothing but her freedom and a fear of motherhood.

His voice when he spoke, his silence, what this did to her: love.

ᔕᔕ

"Time is an old man without ears, just a long beard where pigeons live."

So says Christophe, who fancies himself a poet, though when he writes she's not sure. He fancies many things. That God is time, being old, God is late. Too late.

"Or he has come and gone," she said.

He chuckled, "Yes, perhaps."

If portraits speak they speak the way Christophe does, in metaphors of personal obsessions, distinct as wrinkles which root the features. In Christophe's face: time and pigeons.

"Sorry I'm late. I forgot about spring leap." He's always late. "Time for the pigeons to start going at it," and he looks at her. It is spring. Birds mate in spring. She wants to laugh at such a corny line. But if it's corny, it is gentle also, a mating call that melts her.

"Do you think pigeons enjoy it?" Christophe asks.

"What?"

"Begging."

"What's with you and pigeons?"

"Someone I knew liked pigeons."

"Yer ex-lover?"

"Ya."

Portraits come alive in shadows, creases, by catching what the years have done or haven't done to the child. Christophe, the self-conscious immigrant boy who hammered at English to build an inscrutable mask; a mask now marked by years of drugs, indifference and, round the eyes, by weariness.

Christophe, who left home at the age of sixteen to discover the North American continent, came to Montreal in 1967. "Too early," he says, "since then I've made it my policy to be late." Too early for what?

Early enough to see the Westmount mailboxes explode? To feel the panic in the streets, excitement in a revolution against years of silence? Young enough to believe in change and naive enough to be struck dumb by the October crisis?

But all he said was, "The ancient Greeks had the right idea. When there was no justification for cruelty, murder, or rape, they invented another God."

Christophe speaks the way a portrait does, in codes of silence.

BIOGRAPHIES

ARDIZZI, MARIA

Maria Ardizzi was born in Leognano (Teramo), Italy, where she spent her childhood. She studied in Rome and came to Canada in 1954. In 1980 her novel, *Made in Italy*, won the Ontario Arts Council Literary Competition. In 1982 it was published simultaneously in Italian and English. She has published articles and short stories in various newspapers and magazines. Recently, she completed another novel.

- *Made in Italy*, a novel, Toronto: Toma Publishing Inc., 1980. Reprint due by Guernica in 1998.
- *Made in Italy*, published simultaneously in Italian and English, 1982.
- *Il Sapore Agro della mia Terra*, in Italian, Toronto: Toma Publishing Inc., 1984.
- *Conversasione col figlio*, in Italian and English, Toronto: Toma Publishing Inc., 1985.
- *La Buona America*, in Italian, Toronto: Toma Publishing Inc., 1987.
- *Tra le colline e al di la del Mare*, poetry in Italian, Toronto: Toma Publishing Inc., 1990.
- "A Summer's Dream," a short story, in *Gamut*.

BALDASSARRE, ANGELA

Angela Baldassarre was born in Toronto. At the age of ten she moved with her family to Avellino, Italy where she graduated from High School. They returned to Canada in 1975. While in university she began writing for the school newspaper. Later, she wrote for various music magazines in Toronto and for six years was the only female rock critic in the city. She contributed regularly to such publications as *Shades, New York Rocker,* and *Cream*. She has interviewed musicians such as U2, the Troggs, David Bowie, and Duran Duran. In 1982 she moved to Milan,

Italy to work for Berlusconi's Canale 5 then returned to Toronto in 1984 and a job as senior editor at the newly founded Telelatino Network. Later, she began freelance writing for a variety of newspapers and magazines as well as hosting a live theater show for CKLN. She occasionally teaches a film course for the Learning Annex and continues to write for Canadian and American publications.

- Has contributed music reviews to *Shades, New York Rocker* and *Cream.* Has held the following positions: senior editor at Toronto's Telelatino Network, Managing Editor for a weekly movie magazine, *Showtimes,* Entertainment Editor for *Eye Weekly.* She is movie editor for the London, Ontario *Scene Magazine* and Toronto monthly *Metro Word.* Edits a teen magazine, *Pop Life* and a music magazine, *CD Plus.* She is a regular contributor to *Menz Magazine, Entertainment Weekly, Tribute, Globe and Mail,* as well as other Canadian and American publications.

BECCARELLI-SAAD, TIZIANA

Tziana Beccarelli Saas was born in Como, Italy, and emigrated to Canada after living some years in France. She grew up in Montreal and has a French education with degrees from the Université de Montréal.

- *Les passantes,* Les éditions Triptyque, 1986.
- *Vers l'Amérique,* Les éditions Triptyque, 1988.
- *Les mensonges blancs,* Les éditions Triptyque, 1992.

CANTON, LICIA

Licia Canton has a Ph.D. in Canadian Literature from Université de Montréal. She has written on Frank Paci, Caterina Edwards, Mary Melfi, Nino Ricci and Antonio D'Alfonso. She co-organized the conference titled The Third Solitude: Canadian Minority Writing (Montreal, March 1998) and is presently co-editing a collection of critical essays originally presented at the conference.

COLALILLO-KATZ, ISABELLA

Isabella Colalillo-Katz was born in Boiano, Campobasso, Italy in 1948. She came to Canada in 1956. She is a poet, storyteller, editor and holistic educator living in Toronto. Her poems and articles have been published in a variety of journals and anthologies.

- "Walking up Fifth Avenue," a poem, *Pax: International Journal of Art, Science and Philosophy,* San Antonio, Texas: ed. Bryce Milligan, Winter, 1985.
- "To Dante From 1981, a poem, *Undercurrents: A Journal of Critical Environmental Studies,* Vol.11, 1990, Toronto.
- "On the Death of a Student," an article, *Journal of Among Teachers Community,* No.17, 1995. (Joint Centre for Teacher Development) Faculty of Education, OISE, Toronto.

DAVID, CAROLE

Carole David was born in Montreal and is of Molisan background. She has had numerous publications in a variety of genres: poetry, literary criticism, a novel, newspaper and magazine articles. In 1986 she won the prix Émile-Nelligan for her first collection of poetry, *Terroristes d'amour.* In 1994, her first novel, *Impala* — now translated into English — was a finalist in both the Prix du Journal de Montréal and the Grand Prix du livre de Montréal. She teaches in Montreal and continues to write.

- *Terroristes d'amour,* poetry, Montréal: VLB éditeur, 1986.
- L'endroit où se trouve ton âme, short fictions, Montréal: Éditions Les Herbes rouges, 1991.
- *Feu vers l'est,* poetry in collaboration with Jean-Sébastien Huot, Montréal: Gaz moutarde, 1992.
- *Impala,* a novel, Montréal: Éditions Les Herbes rouges, 1994.
- *Abandons,* Montréal: Editions Les Herbes rouges, 1996.
- *Impala,* English translation by Daniel Sloate, Toronto: Guernica Editions, 1997.
- Reviews, articles, anthologies:
- "La voix noire de Jayme Anne Phillips," revue *Voir,* cahier livres, September, 1995.

- "Art poétique," *Le Sabord,* Fall-Winter, 1996.
- "Sujet délicat," *Estuaire,* Winter, 1996.

DE FRANCESCHI, MARISA

Marisa De Franceschi was born in Muris (Udine), Italy. She came to Canada in 1948 and grew up in Windsor, Ontario where she graduated from the University of Windsor and taught for a number of years. Her short stories, articles, and book reviews have appeared in a variety of Canadian publications including, *Canadian Author & Bookman* and *The Mystery Review.* Her work has appeared in a number of anthologies and she has twice been the recipient of the Okanagan Short Story Award. *Surface Tension* was her first novel. She has completed a second and is working on a third.

- "The Providers," a short story, *Canadian Author & Bookman*, 1980.
- *Stories About Real People, a series of readers,* Mardan Publishing, 1982.
- "Royal Blood," a short story, *Canadian Author & Bookman,* 1984.
- "The Providers" and "Royal Blood" were included in the anthology *Pure Fiction,* Fitzhenry & Whiteside, 1986.
- "Peonies Trying to Survive," a short story, *Ricordi: Things Remembered*, Toronto: Guernica Editions, 1989.
- *Surface Tension,* a novel, Toronto: Guernica Editions, 1994.
- "Things Remembered," a short story, *Investigating Women,* Toronto: Simon & Pierre, 1995.
- Book Reviews for *Canadian Author & Bookman, The Mystery Review, The Windsor Star* and numerous newspaper and magazine articles for a variety of Canadian publications.

DE LUCA CALCE, FIORELLA

Fiorella De Luca Calce was born in (Rocca d'Evandro) Caserta, Italy in 1963. She immigrated to Montreal with her parents at the age of four. She attended John F. Kennedy High School and continued her collegial studies at Vanier College. Recently married, she is juggling a career at Vanier College and pursuing a certificate program at Concordia University as well as writing. Her first novel, *Toni*, has been translated into French and published in the U.K. as *It's a Bloody Girl*. Her most recent novel, *Vinnie and Me*, has also been translated into French.

- "Pomegranate Blossoms," a short story, *Ricordi:Things Remembered*, Toronto: Guernica Editions, 1989.
- *Toni*, a novel, Toronto: Guernica Editions, 1990.
- *Toni,* French translation, Montréal: Les Éditions Balzac, 1994.
- *It's a Bloody Girl,* a novel, formerly published as *Toni*, U.K.: Women's Press, 1991.
- *Vinnie and Me,* a novel, Toronto: Guernica Editions, 1996.

DE SANTIS, DELIA

Delia De Santis was born in Atina, Frosinone, in the region of Lazio. She came to Canada in the 1950s and presently lives with her husband in Bright's Grove, Ontario. Her short stories have appeared in literary magazines and anthologies in Canada and the United States. She received an award from New Day Publications, an American Literary Journal, and another from the Alberta Poetry Yearbook.

- "Night Visitors," a short story, *Western Producer,* 1977.
- "Blueberry Muffins," a short story, *The Ecphorizer,* 1987, and *Voices of the Rapids,* 1993.
- "Dinner For Three," a short story, *Sands of Huron,* Sarnia, 1990.
- "The Colour Red," a short story, *High Profile*, London, Ontario, 1987 and *Renegade,* 1991.
- "Faces in the Window," a short story, *Mind in Motion,* 1985 and *Flare-Up,* 1986.

DI MICHELE, MARY

Mary di Michele is a poet and novelist born in Lanciano, Italy in 1949. Her family immigrated to Toronto in 1955. An associate professor teaching in the English department and creative writing program at Concordia University, she now lives in Montreal.

- *Tree of August,* Toronto: Three Trees Press, 1978.
- *Bread and Chocolate,* along with Bronwen Wallace, *Marrying into the Family,* Ottawa: Oberon, 1980.
- *Mimosa and Other Poems,* Oakville, Ontario: Mosaic, 1981.
- *Necessary Sugar,* Ottawa: Oberon, 1983.
- *Anything is Possible,* editor, an anthology of women's poetry, Oakville, Ontario: Mosaic, 1984.
- *Immune to Gravity,* Toronto: McClelland & Stewart, 1986.
- *Luminous Emergencies,* Toronto: McClelland & Stewart, 1990.
- *Under My skin*, a novel, Kingston: Quarry Press, 1994.
- *Stranger in You,* Selected Poems and New, Toronto: Oxford University Press, 1995.
- Her poetry has appeared in numerous Canadian publications such as *Canadian Forum, Dalhousie Review, Event, Grain, Malahat Review, University of Windsor Review* and others.
- Her work has been translated into French, Spanish and Italian. "Invitation to Beauty's Rose" is a new poem from the manuscript, *Debriefing the Rose.*

EDWARDS, CATERINA

Caterina Edwards was born in Wellingborough, England to an English father and Italian mother and was raised there and in Alberta. She has had numerous publications including the novel, *The Lion's Mouth.* She has published several short stories in such magazines as *Dandelion. Branching Out* and the *Journal of Canadian Fiction.* Her work has been anthologized in *Ricordi: Things Remembered, More Stories From Western Canada* and others. She recently edited a collection of personal essays entitled *Eating Apples: Knowing Women's Lives* and has completed a new novel, *Deadly Elements.* She lives in Edmonton with her husband and two children where she teaches literature and writes.

- *The Lion's Mouth,* a novel, Edmonton: NeWest Publishers, 1982. Reprinted, Toronto: Guernica Editions, 1993.
- "Master of Arts," a short story, in *The Best of Alberta,* Edmonton: Hurtig Publishers, 1987.
- "Prima Vera," a short story, in *Ricordi: Things Remembered,* Toronto: Guernica Editions, 1989.
- *Homeground,* a play, Toronto: Guernica Editions, 1990.
- "Stella's Night," a short story, in *Alberta Rebound,* Edmonton: NeWest Press, 1990.
- *A Whiter Shade of Pale* and *Becoming Emma,* two novellas, Edmonton: NeWest Publishers, 1992.
- "On a Platter," a short story, in *Boundless Alberta,* Edmonton: NeWest Press, 1993.
- Edited in collaboration with Kay Stewart: *Eating apples: Knowing Women's Lives,* a collection of Personal Essays, Edmonton: NeWest Press, 1994.
- She has also published numerous stories in magazines such as *Dandelion, Branching Out, Journal of Canadian Fiction,* and in the anthologies *Getting Here, The Story so Far, More Stories From Western Canada.*

FOSCHI, ANNA CIAMPOLINI

Anna Foschi Ciampolini was born in Florence, Italy in 1945 and settled in Vancouver in 1981. She has been active in the Italian cultural community as Coordinator of Cultural Affairs and of the Heritage Language School at the Italian Cultural Centre in Vancouver. In 1985 she was co-organizer of The First Conference of Italian-Canadian Writers of Western Canada followed the next year by the First National Conference of Italian-Canadian Writers which she co-organized with the late Dino Minni. She has helped promote Italian-Canadian writers by organizing lecture series, workshops, and publishing an exhaustive number of her interviews with Italian-Canadian writers for the Italian newspaper, *L'Eco d'Italia.* Her work has extended into television and documentary film and she is presently Coordinator of the

Volunteers' Programs for the Vancouver and Lower Mainland Multicultural Family Support Services Society.

- She has published over 400 articles in *L'Eco d'Italia,* including feature articles, arts reviews, interviews, and an ongoing series on Italian-Canadian Writers.
- *Guide to Resources and Services in British Columbia,* Multiculturalism B.C./ Ministry of Provincial Secretary, 1984.
- *Emigrante, Storie, Memorie e Segreti della buona cucina dei nostri pionieri,* Giovanni Bitelli Ed., 1985.
- *Writers in Transition: The Proceedings of the First National Conference of Italian-Canadian Writers,* Dino Minni and Anna Foschi Ciampolini, Editors , Toronto: Guernica Editions, 1992.
- "Starting at Square One" appears in Antonio D'Alfonso's *In Italics: In Defense of Ethnicity,* Toronto: Guernica Editions, 1996.

GOLINI, VERA
Vera Golini came to Canada with her family from central Italy in 1956. She has a Ph.D. in Italian and French Studies from the University of California, Berkeley and since 1975 has been a full time professor of Italian at St. Jerome's University (Waterloo, Ontario). Her research on Italian and Italian-Canadian literatures has appeared in journals, books and anthologies. She is vice-president of the Canadian Society for Italian Studies. She serves on the Board of Governors and the Senate of the University of Waterloo and is the Director of its Women's Studies Program.

MADOTT, DARLENE
Darlene Madott lives in Toronto with her young son. Her short stories have been published in Canadian literary magazines and a collection of her work was published by Oberon Press in 1985. She studied law and is presently a Toronto lawyer but continues to write. For the past five years, she has been working on the

screen play, "Mazilli Shoes," for the Toronto producer, Bernard Zukerman.

- *Bottled Roses,* a collection of short stories, Ottawa: Oberon Press, 1985.
- Some of the stories in this anthology first appeared in such publications as *Aurora: New Canadian Writing, Event, Canadian Forum, Canadian Ethnic Studies,* and *Quarry.*

MELFI, MARY

Mary Melfi was born in Italy and came to Canada in 1957. She is a graduate of Loyola College (Concordia University) and McGill University. Her poetry, plays and stories have appeared in numerous Canadian publications. She has published nine books including the novel, *Infertility Rites.* She has also written a book for young adults, *Ubu, The Witch Who Would Be Rich.* She lives in Montreal with her husband and two children.

- *The Dance, The Cage and The Horse,* Montréal: D Press, 1976.
- *A Queen is Holding a Mummified Cat,* Toronto: Guernica Editions, 1982.
- *A Bride in Three Acts,* Toronto: Guernica Editions, 1983.
- *A Dialogue With Masks,* Oakville, Ontario: Mosaic Press, 1985.
- *The O Canada Poems,* Brandon, Manitoba: Brandon University, 1986.
- *A Season in Beware,* Windsor, Ontario: Black Moss Press, 1989.
- *Infertility Rites,* a novel, Toronto: Guernica Editions, 1991.
- *Ubu, the Witch Who Would be Rich,* Toronto: Doubleday Canada, 1994.
- *Sex Therapy,* a black comedy, Toronto: Guernica Editions, 1996.
- *Foreplay,* loosely based on *A Dialogue with Masks,* Mosaic Press, 1985. Workshopped with Anne Page, Fall 1995.
- *½ Italian,* a comedy in three acts. Workshopped with Anne Page, Summer 1996.

PATRIARCA, GIANNA

Gianna Patriarca was born in Ceprano, Frosinone, in the region of Lazio, Italy. She came to Canada in 1960 with her mother and younger sister to join her father who had emigrated in 1956. Her poetry has been published in numerous literary magazines and journals including: *Fireweed, Poetry Toronto Newsletter, Poetry Canada Review, L'étranger, The Worker, The Eyetalian* and others. In 1995 she was runner-up for the Milton Acorn People's Poetry Award. A graduate of York University, she presently teaches in the Toronto area where she lives with her husband and daughter.

- *Italian Women and Other Tragedies,* a poetry collection, Toronto: Guernica Editions, 1994.
- *Daughters for Sale,* poetry, Toronto: Guernica Editions, 1997.

PERRELLA, FLORENCE

Florence Perella was born in Queens, New York in 1935. She immigrated to Canada in 1978. She received a Bachelor's and Master's of Religious Studies at McGill University and served for a time as chaplain at the McGill Newman Centre. Ms. Perella died the summer of 1996 from the effects of ALS (Lew Gehrig's disease). "Basil and Clementines" was written during the last stages of this terrible illness. She is the mother of four children.

- *Da Bellezza or Beauty* and *My Boundaries* were published privately by Ms. Perella.

PETRONE, PENNY

Penny Petrone was born and raised in Thunder Bay (Port Arthur), Ontario where she still resides. She has taught for nearly fifty years at the elementary, high school, and university levels. She was made an honorary chief of the Gull Bay Ojibway for her pioneering work in Native literature. In 1992, she was awarded the Order of Ontario. She is a Professor Emeritus of Education at Lakehead University.

- *Selected Short Stories of Isabella Valancy Crawford,* Ottawa: University of Ottawa Press, 1975.
- *The Fairy Tales of Isabella Valancy Crawford,* Ottawa: Borealis Press, 1977.
- *First People, First Voices,* Toronto: University of Toronto Press, 1983.
- *Northern Voices: Inuit Writing in English,* Toronto: University of Toronto Press, 1988.
- *Native Literature in Canada,* Toronto: Oxford University Press, 1990.
- *Breaking the Mould,* a memoir, Toronto: Guernica Editions, 1995.

PRINCIPE, CONCETTA

Concetta Principe was born in Toronto in 1964. She completed her Master's Degree in English in the Creative Writing Program at Concordia University. She currently lives and writes in Toronto.
- *Stained Glass,* a novella, Toronto: Guernica Editions, 1996.

STELLIN, MONICA

Although Canadian-born, she spent most of her life in Italy and came back to Canada only recently. Bridging the ocean has become her way of life: she has graduated and taught at both Italian and Canadian universities and dedicated herself to the study of Canadian multiculturalism from an Italian perspective and to the Italian literature of migration to Canada. She now lives in Toronto.

WELCH, LILIANE

Liliane Welch was born in Esch-sur-Alzette, Luxembourg in 1937. She immigrated to Canada in 1967. She has written fourteen collections of poetry, including *Life in Another Language,* which won the Bressani Prize. She has coauthored two volumes of literary criticism on modern French poetry, and has published a book of essays, *Seismographs.* Her writings have been widely

anthologized and translated into French, German and Italian.
Her many honours include the Alfred Bailey Prize. Liliane
Welch teaches at Mount Allison University in Sackville, New
Brunswick. An ardent mountaineer, she climbs each summer in
the Alps and Dolomites.

- *Emergence: Baudelaire, Mallarme, Rimbaud,* with C. Welch, State College, Bald Eagle, 1973.
- *Winter Songs,* poetry, London: Killaly Press, 1977.
- *Syntax of Ferment,* poetry, Fredericton: Fiddlehead Books, 1979.
- *Assailing Beats,* poetry, Ottawa: Borealis, 1979.
- *Address: Rimbaud, Mallarme, Butor,* with C. Welch, Victoria: Sono Nis, 1979.
- *October Winds,* poetry, Fredericton: Fiddlehead Books, 1980.
- *Brush and Trunks,* poetry, Fredericton: Fiddlehead Books, 1981.
- *From the Songs of the Artisans,* poetry, Fredericton: Fiddlehead Books, 1983.
- *Unrest Bound,* poetry, Brandon: Pierian Press, 1985.
- *Manstorna: Life on the Mountain,* poetry, Charlottetown: Ragweed, 1987.
- *Word-House of a Grandchild,* poetry, Charlottetown: Ragweed, 1987.
- *A Taste for Words,* poetry, Saint John: The Purple Wednesday Society, 1988.
- *Seismographs: Selected Essays and Reviews,* Charlottetown: Ragweed, 1988.
- *Fire to the Looms Below,* poetry, Charlottetown: Ragweed, 1990.
- *Life in Another Language,* poetry, Dunvegan: Cormorant, 1992.
- *Von Menschen und Orten,* poetry, Luxembourg: Les Cahiers Luxembourgeois, 1992.
- *Dream Museum,* poetry, Victoria: Sono Nis, 1995.
- *Fidelities,* poetry, Ottawa: Borealis, 1997.

ZAGOLIN, BIANCA

Bianca Zagolin was born in Northern Italy and settled in Montreal at the age of nine. She was schooled in French but chose to complete her B.A. in English. She holds a Ph.D. in French Language and Literature, a field in which she teaches and writes. She has published articles, short stories and a critical essay on Quebec novelist, Marie-Claire Blais. Her first novel, *Une femme à la fenêtre*, was published in Paris in 1988. She has since translated the novel into English. She is now working on a second novel which centers on one of the characters of the first.

- *Une femme à la fenêtre*, a novel, Paris: Editions Robert Laffont, 1988.
- *L'Histoire d'un déracinement*, Les Écrits du Canada Français, Montréal: 1990.
- *Les Métamorohoses de Chloé*, story, *Arcade*, no. 20, Montréal, 1990.
- *Marie-Claire Blais: La Fureur sacrée de la parole, Le Roman contemporain au Québec: 1960-1985*, Les Archives des lettres canadiennes, Tome VIII, Montréal: Fides, 1992.
- "Littérature d'immigration ou littérature tout court?," *Possibles*, Volume 17, no. 2, printemps, 1993.

ZIOLKOWSKI, CARMEN LAURENZA

Carmen Laurenza Ziolkowski was born in Italy. She lived in England for some time where she worked as a registered nurse. In the 1960s she studied journalism at Port Huron College and Wayne State University in Detroit. Her work has been published in Canada, Italy, the U.S. and England. Her short stories have been read on CBC radio and anthologized in such publications as *Polished Pebbles, Flare Up, Sands of Huron, Voices of the Rapids* and *Best Canadian Anecdotes*. She has been involved with the creative writing program at Lampton College. She lives in Sarnia with her husband, Bruno. They have two grown sons and three grandchildren.

- *Roses Bloom at Dusk*, poetry, Vesta Publications, 1976.

- *The House of Four Winds,* Sarnia: River City Press, 1987.
- "Mirabella," a short story, Sands of Huron, 1990.
- "A Memorable Night," anecdote contest, Madiera Park, B.C.: Harbour Publishing, 1991.
- "The Splendor — Threats of Vesuvius," essay, *Voices of the Rapids,* River City Press, 1993.
- *World of Dreams,* poetry, Sarnia: River City Press, 1995.
- "Watermelon is Sweet," a short story, *Flare Up,* River City Press, 1996.

ACKNOWLEDGEMENTS

The editor and publisher express their gratitude to the following for allowing them to reproduce their works in this anthology:

Maria Ardizzi, Anna Maria Castrilli, and Toma Publishing Inc., for the selection from her novel *Made in Italy*, 1980.

Angela Baldassarre for the two previously published interviews.

Tiziana Beccarelli-Saad, Domenic Cusmano and Les éditions Triptyque for the short story taken from *Les passantes*, 1986.

Isabella Colalillo-Katz for the previously unpublished poems.

Carole David, Daniel Sloate, Les Herbes Rouges, and Guernica Editions for the selection from her novel, *Impala*, 1997.

Marisa De Franceschi for the previously unpublished short story.

Fiorella De Luca Calce and Guernica Editions for the selection taken from her novel *Toni*, 1990.

Delia De Santis and *Sands of Huron*, for her story published in 1990, and *High Profile* and *Renegade*, for her story published in 1987 and 1991.

Mary di Michele and Oberon for the selection from *Necessary Sugar*, 1983; the author and Oxford Press for the poem from the *Stranger in You*, 1995; and again the author and McClelland & Stewart for the selection from *Luminous Emergencies*, 1990.

Caterina Edwards for "Stella's Night," previously published in *Alberta Rebound* (NeWest Press, 1990), and again the author and NeWest Publishers and Guernica Editions for the selection from her novel *The Lion's Mouth* (NeWest Publishers, 1982, and Guernica, 1993).

Anna Foschi Ciampolini and *L'Eco d'Italia* for the interviews originally published in Italian in 1989, 1988, and 1990.

Carmen Laurenza Ziolkowski and River City Press, for the selection from *World of Dreams,* 1995.

Darlene Madott for the selection taken from her screenplay, *Mazilli Shoes.*

Mary Melfi and Guernica Editions for the selection from her play, *Sex Therapy,* 1996, and *Office Politics,* forthcoming at Guernica Editions.

Gianna Patriarca and Guernica Editions, for the selections from *Italian Women and Other Tragedies,* 1994, and *Daughters for Sale,* 1997.

Penny Petrone and Guernica Editions, for the selection from *Breaking the Mould,* 1995.

Florence Perrella and her Estate for the selection of her previously unpublished poems.

Concetta Principe and Guernica Editions for the selection from her novella, *Stained Glass,* 1997.

Lilian Welch and Ragweed for the selection from *Seismographs,* 1998, and again the author and Sono Nis, for the selection from *Dream Museum,* 1995.

Bianza Zagolin and les éditions Robert Laffont for the selection from her novel, *Une femme à la fenêtre,* 1988.

PRINTED AND BOUND
IN BOUCHERVILLE, QUÉBEC, CANADA
BY MARC VEILLEUX IMPRIMEUR INC.
IN OCTOBER, 1998